MW00941802

A GINGERSNAP CAT Christmas

Also by Danielle Williams

The Bureaucrat
Growing Shadows in the Desert
Love Potion Commotion!
Out Where the Sun Always Shines
The Purrfect Christmas
What the Cat Brought Back

Available at PixelvaniaPublishing.com

Copyright © 2018 Danielle Williams

All rights reserved. This is a work of fiction. Names, characters, places, and incidents either are the products of the author's imagination or are used fictitiously to convey a sense of realism. Any resemblance to actual persons, living or dead, businesses, companies, events, or locales is entirely coincidental.

Visit the author's website at www.PixelvaniaPublishing.com

Printed in the USA
First Printing, 2018
ISBN: 978-1-7326308-2-6

For Cassidy and Dominique
and the members of the Monte Cristo ward, our angels
when we needed them.

"I believe cats to be spirits come to earth. A cat, I am sure, could walk on a cloud without coming through."

—*Jules Verne*

"Where there is great love there are always miracles."

—*Willa Cather*

A GINGERSNAP CAT Christmas

DANIELLE WILLIAMS

PIXELVANIA PUBLISHING

CHAPTER ONE

My name is Gingersnap. I used to live on Earth with my family, but like all animals do, I got old and died. I live in Heaven now, in Cat Housing (domesticated division). I'll move over to the Human development when my forever family makes it up here. Right now only my master's mom and dad are up here, but they're dog people. They live with Sammy, their Chihuahua. I still visit twice a year, but it's not the same without my forever family.

Some of my cat friends live over in the Human development right now, even if it's just part time, but I was with the Romanos a long time, and I'd feel strange hanging around other humans. I mean, I spent some time on the streets, but when I finally found my forever family, I *fit*, snug as a mouse in its hole, or like one of those pieces in a jigsaw puzzle, like my Gina used to do.

(Sometimes at night I'd get bored and play with the loose pieces. Luckily, Damien, Gina's dad, was a smart guy and made a scraper out of a long stick so she could sweep 'em out from under the sofa where I usually wound up batting them. Hey, instinct's instinct.)

Anyway, Cat Housing's really great. It's sunny, there are trees everywhere—bare *and* leafed—no cars or vacuums, and some of the smarter rats (and mice, and voles, etc.) agreed to start a community hunting league, where they try to outsmart us while we chase them. But no one ever dies up here. Of course. Everyone touches noses after and goes home. It's a good team sport. I hear they're even trying to get a Birding league started.

Heaven is terrific.

But this year...I dunno. I can't say I'm bored—I'm a cat, sleeping's still one of my favorite hobbies—but something's just...*missing*.

CHAPTER TWO

"*Psst.* Gingersnap. Gingersnap. Hey, Gingie!"

Rodney, my Siamese friend, butted his head into my shoulder.

"What?" I rolled awake. "And don't call me Gingie!"

"Sorry," he said, but his brown tail still waved in the air, so I knew he wasn't. "But you know how you've been moping around, saying you want something to do?"

"Yes, I am aware of the things I have said."

He rolled his blue eyes. "Well, Feather's calling for some extra paws to help with the Christmas decorations this year. You should come!"

"Right now?"

"Yeah!"

I licked my paw—first to wash my face and wake me up a little more, second to buy me some time.

3

Christmas in Heaven is a Big Deal; everyone here goes all out. My buddy George had been on the decorating team every year and loved it, but collecting and transporting doodads was in his bones. He told me once about a time he'd brought his person back a slipper big as he was, back on Earth when he was just a kitten.

Hoarding'd never been my scene. But if it could fill up the hole that was inside me...well, it'd be worth a short.

I stretched slowly, trying not to look too eager. Rodney already had enough eagerness for four cats.

"Goodie!" he said as I stepped off my sleeping platform. He turned and trotted to the tree trunk. After a second to lick my ears presentable, I followed him.

Heaven's cat colony shared a lot of giant trees like this. The trunks are thick and delicious to scratch, the branches are sturdy, and at the ends of some of the limbs are wooden-plank platforms (well, mine came with carpet) where a cat can sleep and keep an eye on things.

Even though there's no roofs on our boxes, the setup reminds me of the treehouse my Damien built for Gina. We used to do a lot of reading up there. Once I was even the special guest at one of her birthday slumber parties. I snuck a lot of dried pizza cheese that night!

My exotic shorthair friend Mel, though, he lives in a super-sized carpeted cat condo between Cat Housing and the human development. And my moggie friend Julia-Goolia lives in a barn.

I greeted my neighbors with tail waves as I backed down the tree after Rodney. Near the bottom, I leapt onto the grass and clawed my own mark into the satisfyingly ragged base of the tree trunk. Then I followed Rodney. I hoped this decorating thing was worth interrupting my nap.

CHAPTER THREE

In the distance I could see a huge cardboard box, big as a house, but with no roof. Inside, smaller, more reasonably-sized boxes stood at regular intervals. Cats were trotting up to the smaller boxes, reaching in, and grabbing out different objects before leaving the superbox.

A line of them were heading in me and Rodney's direction, some with decorations in their mouths or wound around their tails.

George the hoarder suddenly appeared on top of the hill with us, heading in our direction. Spotting me, he trotted over. He set the bauble in his mouth down in the grass. At first I thought it was a snowman, since it was white and fuzzy. But then I saw it was a fuzzy toy lamb, a little bigger than a baby bird.

George touched noses with me.

"Gingersnap! I didn't think you'd come!"

"Yeah, well, Rodney invited me, and you know I can't say no to that long face."

George and I chuckled at the joke, but Rodney heard it, so he whapped me in the face with his tail.

"I know you're jealous of my exotic bone structure," he said, "but that's no reason to be catty."

"What's that for?" I nodded down at the lamb.

George beamed. "It's for the Christmas tree outside of the barn in Cleanwhisker. The theme this year is 'lions and lambs'!"

"Ooh, that's a GREAT theme!" said Rodney.

I nodded. "Definitely."

"Here." He rolled the lamb towards me with his nose. "You can take my lamb up the tree. I'll go back to the supply box and grab another."

"Okay," I said. "But where—" I turned my head, distracted by a sandy-colored queen cat trotting by. Her tail was held high; trailing from it was a narrow banner of lights, floating in midair. Miniature suns, and it was all I could do not to bat at them.

"Yeah!" George trilluped. "Just follow her. Those are for our tree."

"...Right," I said. I picked up the lamb in my mouth. Woolly, but not unpleasant.

"Great! See you inna bit!" said George, and he bounded back towards the giant supply box.

"Come on, Gingersnap. We don't wanna lose her!"

Rodney took off after the queen cat with the lights, and so did I.

She was a straggler following a clump of a dozen cats, some holding fuzzy lambs in their mouths, others miniature (but still very handsome) lion figures. Floating lights drifted off the tips of other upright tails like streamers.

Some people think heaven is made of fluffy white clouds. Maybe it is over in the bird section, but in Cat Housing, the ground is soft green grass (with only some of it grown out tall enough to tickle your belly) and forests...and even a beach, though I'd never felt the need to visit. Sand belongs in a box, if you ask me.

Me and Rodney joined the decorators arching into the pine forest, sometimes resisting the urge to pounce on the floating lights; other times spooking as the lights' movement threw the pine needles' shapes into crazy shadows. We followed the group until the land opened out again. There was the Cleanwhisker barn, bright red. In front of it, an unleapable pine tree—taller than the barn itself—stood just outside the front door, like it had grown up overnight. Cats of all kinds were crawling over the tree. The rust-orange rump of a tabby cousin disappeared beneath the green limbs. Seconds later, a paw batted out, adjusting the drape of a string of sun-lights.

"Wow! Lookit, Gingersnap!" Rodney leapt into the air. Our traveling partners dove away from his Outside Voice.

I nodded my head. This small little thing in my mouth was supposed to go on such a big tree? Who would ever see it? Near the bottom, noble lion masks—golden, carved by human hands—faced out in every direction.

The sandy queen with the lights streaming from her tail broke into a run. The lights followed like chasing fireflies.

We all ran to keep up with her.

* * *

At the base of the tree, everyone seemed to be milling about a tiny tortoiseshell cat.

"You, squirrel level," she said, tapping a tom with her paw. He strutted out of the group and up the tree.

I sighed through my sheep. It had to be a Tortie.

"I hear ya," said Rodney, "but hey, the tree *does* look good."

I looked up at the tree again. It was true. Even though all the decorations weren't up, the lion faces shone magnificently in the light, and some, reflecting the barn, turned the chocolate-red color of a Havana brown.

I hustled down the hill and into the circling river of fur surrounding the Tortie. I thought I'd have time to meander with the crowd, but, spotting me, her amber eyes bulged.

"Hey, you! Ginger with the sheep! Yes, you!"

I lashed my tail. Darn.

"That's the first one," she said, approaching me. "The first sheep. They'll be going on the middle part of the tree. You can put it anywhere between blue jay level and cardinal level. No higher than cardinal!" She batted the air for emphasis.

I set the sheep carefully down on my paws. There was no dirt in heaven, but I thought she might split a whisker if I put it on the ground.

"How's anybody going to see something so small so high up?"

"Because it's not going to stay small. When you get up there, lick its back, then bop it with your paw, like this!"

She demonstrated on the back of a kitten who just darted by. He put on the brakes and spun around, trying to find the perpetrator, only to be pounced on by his siblings. The Tortie recoiled in surprise.

"Kittens! Out of the way, unless you're helping!"

One of them looked up, indignant. "We are!"

I left the kitten to argue with her, grabbing my sheep and ducking under the green-needled branches.

Most people don't know that Heaven is made of light—so much so that even the shadows aren't truly dark. But beneath the branches everything I saw was tinted piney green and dark purple. I dug my claws into the trunk—past the picture of the button, and began climbing.

Every few tail lengths a picture was attached to the trunk. It wasn't the tallest tree I'd ever climbed in Heaven—this Christmas tree wasn't half as big as the tree I lived on—but inside the green tunnel of the tree's body, it felt like a long time passed before I got anywhere.

"'Scuze me, going down," said a calico queen at squirrel level. I scooched aside so she could descend.

"Those masks are heavy!" I heard her say down below my tail. I heard voices behind me as I climbed, but none of them ever tried to push past me, and I didn't see anyone ahead of me, going up or trying to go down. If I was the first sheep, maybe I was the first one up to blue jay level? Did the Tortie plan it that way?

Some cats are too smart for their own good.

I kept climbing.

Finally, I saw the blue bird with the pointy head and frowny beak. Blue jay level.

Might as well get off here. I left the trunk and made my way to the end of the branch.

I frowned around my decoration. I could probably find a place to set it down, but if I bopped it, it was going to fall through the branches and get stuck farther down, and the Tortie wouldn't like that. Worse, it might hit the ground, and she REALLY wouldn't like that.

Even though cats aren't mean in Heaven, some are still prone to annoying lectures.

I looked around. The views were good—I thought I could see my home tree, a blueish gray shape in the distance.

But I can't go home without dropping off this silly sheep!

I sat down and began searching the branches below me. From time to time heads and paws pushed through the needles as cats attached ornaments—somehow!—to the tree.

My tail lashed. The Tortie could have given me better instructions.

"Hey!"

"Careful!"

"Slow down!"

Cats in the tree below me began shouting, and branches rustled, the disturbance preceding the giggles of young kittens.

Oh, brother. I hurried back to the trunk and dug my claws in. Kittens were OK, but I didn't need their rambunctiousness knocking me out of the tree. It would be undignified.

I watched the branches shiver. I heard the giggles growing closer. And I even thought I heard the Tortie yowling up the tree.

Sure enough, the squirm of kittens made it to blue jay level. They chased each other through the pine's undergrowth, so close to one another that they might as well have been a single ribbon of fur and stripes. One's white foot thwacked me in the nose as he flew by. I flinched, but didn't drop the sheep.

"Sorry!" said the kitten. Then, he dropped out of the careening chase and landed in front of me, on a different branch connected to the trunk. It was the kitten from down below, all white except for a triangular patch growing between his ears, and a little gray saddle on his back that turned his tail gray, too.

"What's up?" he said. "You haven't put your ornament on."

I turned around in a circle.

"Oh, you don't know how?" he said. "It's easy, I'll show you."

He stepped onto my branch and brushed past me.

Things in Heaven aren't as solid as they are back on Earth. While I can feel the tree limb underfoot, there's something not-quite-the-same about it. Like, the surface of it isn't as solid as my foot-whiskers tell me it should be. And even though I can feel, say, Rodney's tongue when he gives me a friendly lick, the texture's just not quite *there*.

But when the kitten brushed by, he felt like a dream—or like a thin covering of fur over a cloud.

Why, he hasn't been born yet!

I wanted to ask him a question—he was the first cat I'd met who hadn't been to Earth already—but he was at the end of the branch, looking over his shoulder at me. I walked out to him. He scooped his paw under the branch and when he brought it back up, there was a metal ball in it, the same color as the lion heads, big as a Main Coon's paw.

"Okay, so these are on every branch," he said. Now that he'd pointed them out to me, I saw them above me, too, dangling from the branch the next level up.

"If you hold your ornament against it for a few seconds, it'll float there when you let go. Though I don't see how anyone's gonna see your drooly woolly all the way up here!"

Just wait, kit.

I sat up on my haunches and pulled one of the balls above me towards my face. I stuck my neck out and felt the sheep push against the metal ball. I froze in place for a slow blink, then s-l-o-o-o-w-ly relaxed my jaws.

To my relief, the lamb didn't fall! It floated below the metal ball, a toe's length of space around it.

Heaven! Go figure.

I batted the lamb with my paw. It swung as though attached to the ball with a string.

"Thanks, kit. How does it come off?"

His tail crooked. "Dunno. That's for the takedown crew. 'Many paws make light work', and all."

"Got it."

I sat up again, licked the lamb's back, then gave it a good paw-bop.

POUF!

It exploded like popcorn popping and me and the kit both dove for cover by the trunk. Then, after my tail had smoothed back down to its normal size, we clambered back out on the limb to see what had happened.

What had been the size of a mouse in my mouth was now twice the size of a lion mask, a trio of sheep looked to be sleeping in a pile.

"Cool!" said the kitten. "Did you know it was going to do that?"

"Just following orders," I said.

Giggling made our ears twitch upwards. His future siblings zoomed down the branches behind us.

"Gotta go!" said the white-and-gray kitten, and he leapt to join the ribbon of hyperactivity. I was out on a limb alone again.

That wasn't too bad.

I went back to the trunk. Time to get another ornament.

The kitten's comment wasn't the first time I'd heard *many paws make light work*. Having not really done much work on Earth, I finally asked Sammy about it, and he explained that it meant if a group of animals did a big job together instead of alone, it usually got done faster and easier.

I'd filed the explanation away and hadn't thought about it since then. But when I saw the clowder of cats at the foot of the tree after putting up my lambs, the phrase floated through my head again. But there was still a question mark at the end of the saying until my third trip from the supply box.

I stood on the hill looking at the tree. It looked done already! The lions still gleamed at the bottom, and fuzzy sheep families peppered the tree like bits of oversized fuzz. Near the top, a pair of ragdoll cats were unwinding a blue ribbon with a scene of lions and sheep napping together. The tip-top of the tree was coned with a lion wearing a starred crown.

Suddenly, the blue shiny I was carrying didn't seem all that important. I would have left it there on the hill, except I didn't need the Tortie grousing at me. When I took it to her, there were only three cats around her. The rest were padding off to the barn loft to admire their work.

The Tortie saw my shiny. "Find an empty spot in button row and stick it in. It's looking a little bare through there."

Of course, you didn't have to climb the tree at all to reach button level; it was the lowest level of branches. I circled the tree until I found a single spot open on a branch, facing the barn. I stuck the shiny on.

I stepped back a ways and sat down, wrapping my tail around my paws. Among limbs packed with lights, lions, and shinies, my blue shiny had made little difference. But I'd put on other things—the lambs, and an extra floating thing. Those had made a difference, hadn't they?

Tail-tip wagging, I went up to the barn loft to join the other cats.

CHAPTER FOUR

The hay in the loft was clean, what little of it I could see between the paws of the different cats. The walls were warm-wood brown and a square window let in bright light, framing the Christmas tree outside. The resident cats called down to their friends from their specially-built perches up above in the rafters. But from the scent of them, most of the cats pushing towards the square window were from other places, come down to decorate.

"Gingersnap! Over here!"

My ear twitched, and then my eyes followed the voice. George sat on his haunches so I could see his round face above the crowd.

"'Scuze me," I said, and darted through the mass of excited cats. Just as I got to George, Rodney popped up next to him, blue eyes wide with excitement. He sniffed the air over the clowder.

17

"You seen the tree yet, Gingersnap?" asked George.

"No, I just got inside," I said.

"We'll help you get through," said Rodney. "OUTTA THE WAY! OFFICIAL DECORATORS COMIN' THROUGH!" He continued yelling as we pushed our way towards the window. Cats rolled their eyes at his brash cries (I thought I heard someone say, "We're ALL decorators!") but moved aside.

I blinked hard in the dazzling light. The window was level with some fuzzy lambs and paw-print-shaped shinies. My sheep pile might have been on this level, but even if it was, it was on the opposite side of the tree.

"Aw, wow! Wow!" said Rodney. George's tail swirled through the air, pleased.

"Yeah, isn't it a great theme? Those paw shapes are from real lions over in Big Cat Housing!"

"How'd they make them?" I asked. I'd seen my paws make tracks in mud before, but these were shiny and smooth.

George shrugged. "Dunno. Humans and...molds? But not, like, yucky molds." His tail covered his face in distaste.

"It's beautiful," I said. And it was, but looking at it made me feel alone, even sitting with my friends. Our Christmas tree had been small, plastic, but full of bright lights that changed color every few seconds. But it wasn't the tree so much. There'd be wrapping to play in Christmas morning in Heaven, but no Gina there to dangle the ribbon. No Damien to offer me a shoe or slipper box. No Marie to take flashing pictures with her hand rectangle. That's what I missed.

Come on, Gingersnap. It's the season to celebrate the Lord's birthday, not mope around about things you can't change.

I put on a better smile and turned to my friends. A glance passed between them—but I didn't catch what kind. "Yeah. I like it. It's real nice."

* * *

That night at my tree, I settled in to my box. From here I could just make out the glow of Cleanwhisker barn's Christmas tree. But I couldn't sleep.

When you live in Heaven, you can see almost all the stars. Once, when I was on Earth, there was a hole and Gina spilled rice on the floor. There had been too many to play with, too many to count! I'd never seen so many of one thing in my entire life on Earth.

But the stars you can see in Heaven—there's more of them than all the rice anywhere!

Whenever I couldn't sleep, I'd set my chin on the edge of my box and try counting the stars. But tonight, counting didn't interest me.

It had felt good to work on the tree. When I was fetching the shinies and placing them on the branches, I forgot about being a missing piece. I stopped wondering when the rest of my family would be up here so I could live with them again.

I liked my friends—Rodney and George and Julia-Goolia— I liked most all the cats I'd met up here, really. And it was fine visiting Grandma and Grandpa and Sammy. But—maybe— wasn't there something else?

My tail lashed.

Leave it to you to be unhappy in Heaven, Gingersnap.

No, I'd go down tomorrow and help decorate the next thing for Christmas. Rumor in the barn loft was that the cat condos were going to have a Christmas tree full of doves. I could do doves.

I'd decorate the rest of the year, join the yearly Midnight Rally on Christmas Eve to listen to the Nativity donkey tell us what happened that night in the stable...and then...and then...

I smushed my face into the dark corner of my box.

I'll think about that later.

CHAPTER FIVE

When I woke up, it was still dark (or at least, as dark as it ever got in Heaven with the shining rice-spill of stars). My box didn't feel as comfortable as it usually did, but it was way too early to head to the decorating supplies.

My tail lashed. The missing piece feeling was starting to creep back in...

"Gingersnap."

My ears perked up. The voice hadn't been loud, but I'd heard it, clear as water.

"Gingersnap."

I stood up. No cat around me was stirring.

"Gingersnap, come down."

I looked down. Then I saw Him.

My fur puffed out, and I raced down the tree so fast you would have thought I was a squirrel.

He was waiting for me at the foot of the tree, bent down, arms wide to receive me.

I ran towards Him as fast as I could.

"My Lord!" I shouted.

I leaped, and He caught me in His arms and cuddled me. It felt like being wrapped in a purr.

I don't think anybody can really describe our Lord to you if you haven't seen Him before. The least you should know is this: his eyes are *kind*. And His arms feel safe and strong.

He rubbed my head in the middle of my brow, the good spot.

"Good morning, Gingersnap."

I couldn't do anything but purr, but He understood.

"Your friends are worried about you, Gingersnap. They've sent prayers to Me. I know you're missing your family, Gingersnap."

I nodded, suddenly filled with all the sadness you get when you have so many good memories of someone. Only I had many someones: Damien, who got me out of the shelter and never took me back, even though I'd only eat fries and buns and milkshakes at first; his mate Marie, who said she wasn't crazy about me but who checked on me twice a night before my final trip to the vet... and Gina, their daughter, who I saw going off to school every day on the bus when she was a girl, and then only a few times a year when she went off to that town called College.

"Heaven's good, my Lord," I said. "Don't be mad. But I miss them so much!"

He just held me while I missed them and hurt. It was OK to be sad with Him. Then I thought I heard him sniffle and felt embarrassed.

"Sorry, Lord. I know I'm just a cat." I didn't know what else to add after that.

"Oh...dear Gingersnap," He said, and stroked my face. I sighed.

He sat there in Heaven's grass with me in His arms. I don't know how long we were there. Finally, he spoke again.

"Your family has missions on Earth that they must complete before I call them home, Gingersnap. But I don't want you to be unhappy while you wait for them. Do you know what a calling is, Gingersnap?"

"No, Lord."

"It's like an invitation."

I thought about it. "An invitation to another Housing?"

"No," he said gently. "It's an invitation to serve."

"Serve?"

"Yes. Serve. Service is like work."

"Work? Like a dog?" Pictures of leading blind humans around and sniffing human luggage at the airport flew into my head. Then I heard the way I'd said it and wished my tail were thick enough to hide in.

But He didn't get mad. Instead, He laughed, but in a nice way. A reassuring laugh.

"No, not like a dog, not at all. When you serve in this calling, you don't have to be anyone different than you already are, Gingersnap Cat."

"Oh. Okay." My tail swished once, then I stopped it. "You're inviting me to serve? What will I have to do?"

"Guide alley cats to the families I need them to be in."

"Hm." My tail swished again. "Like that tour cat who met me at the Rainbow Bridge?"

He was smiling like He was trying not to laugh. "No. You'll be one of my angels, performing your mission back on Earth."

My fur puffed. "On Earth?! I don't have to be a kitten again, do I?"

"No, Gingersnap. You'll go back fully grown, like you are now."

"Oh." My tail swished a third time. He kissed my head and I felt better.

I hadn't heard of any cats going back. Would that make me a ghost? Would I remember Heaven and all my friends here?

"The cats I will send you to need your help, Gingersnap. You know how to survive without humans, but you're not afraid of them. You can teach the alley cats how to be near humans so they feel comfortable, and keep them safe until they're adopted off the street."

He says they need my help.

We sat there awhile again. The stars were beginning to disappear, blending into the brighter light of the sun.

"Do you accept this calling to help street cats, Gingersnap?"

I looked into His kind face again.

"Yes, my Lord."

He set his warm palm on my head. It seemed to tremble a moment. Then he removed it and gave me a kiss on the nose.

"Thank you, Gingersnap. You're going to do great!"

He set me down on the grass and leaned in. He pointed towards a sunny hill I'd never visited before.

"Go that way," He said, "when you're ready to get started."

I butted His hand with my head to say thank you and set off towards the sunny hill.

CHAPTER SIX

The sunny hill was a lot farther away than it looked. It was almost midmorning when I reached the top. There wasn't anything close by it—and you'd know, because it was a high hill with a killer view. But everything I could see—from my sleeping tree to Cleanwhisker barn—was fly-sized, and hard to make out in the distance.

I plunked down on the hilltop, scenting the air out of habit, not sure where to go next. My paws twitched. I wanted to get going on my mission, not stand out here in the middle of nowhere!

I turned around in a circle and yowled. Where did I go from here?

Rustle, rustle.

I hopped around to face the noise. A familiar brown-masked, blue-eyed face peeked up over the hill.

"Rodney?" I said. "What are you doing out here?"

He bounced onto the hilltop, smiling. Then, after a second, he pounced on me and we wrestled for a few minutes. Afterwards, while we panted, he answered, "I had a dream early this morning," he said. "One of those Heaven dreams. It told me to come up here today and that I'd meet a cat and take him to the Hamper Hills. But I had no idea it'd be you, Gingersnap!"

"Hamper Hills? Where's that?"

"I'll show you!" he said. I followed him off the hill.

I loved Rodney, so I didn't tune out his chatter about the progress they'd made with the Birding league until fifteen minutes in. By the time we were coming out of the Etched Woods, he'd moved on to classic cat jokes.

"Why do cat guardians get on the news more often than dog owners? ...Go on, Gin, guess!"

"I don't know, Rodney, why?"

"'Cuz they're better at getting the SCOOP! Get it?"

I liked his love of the joke more than I liked the joke, which helped me chuckle.

"Oh, hey, we're here!" he said.

The sky was getting dim, but the Hamper Hills shone in the twilight. I sniffed, inhaling the faint scent of fabric softener. The Hamper Hills were mounds and mounds of clean human clothing—mostly white, but in some spots other colors were sprinkled in like wildflowers. The mounds reached into the sky, almost touching the stars that were beginning to twinkle. Cats sat at the top of each mound, talking with each other. Something seemed different about them.

Rodney brushed my shoulder with his head.

"You're leaving?" I asked. He was already looking over his shoulder at me, facing the woods.

"Yep. I hear you're due at the tippy-top by moonrise, so you better shake a whisker!"

"What happens next?"

"Dunno. Figured you'd have all the instructions!"

His grin dropped and he turned around. He nuzzled my cheek again. "Hey, you'll be all right!"

This was Heaven, so I knew he was right, but all the same, I didn't want to climb the hills alone. All the cats up there looked like they belonged. I felt like a shelter kitten.

"Oh, Ginge, come on! A little excitement is what you need."

He was right again. I started to tell him to go on back, but then he sprang up with a waul.

"All right, softiepaw, I'll come up with you! But I'm not speaking to her!"

Someone a Siamese wouldn't talk to? My tail curled, intrigued. "Who?"

"Never mind," he said, and shot past me up the first squishy hill.

All the laundry was warm. Now I felt silly for being a fraidy cat at the bottom. The cats on the laundry piles were just as relaxed and lifted their chins and tails in friendly hellos as we climbed.

The sun went away and the stars came out, but the warm laundry seemed to glow. I thought it would be a harder climb, what with there being nothing compressing the socks and shirts together, but enough cats had been through here that their paws tamped down a way sturdy as any garden path.

Me and Rodney were shoulder to shoulder when we reached the summit.

"What do you think they do up here?" he asked.

I shrugged.

Waiting for us was a soft-pelted bobtail cat with a glowing collar around her neck. It looked like it could have been made out of the bright moon behind her, a single smooth shape. Rodney, who had been telling me about his human's clothes on Earth, muttered, "Oh good, it isn't her."

The bobtail leapt in front of me in one bound. Her shaggy shock of a tail wagged. "Are you Gingersnap?" she said. "You must be. There's not a lot of time before you go back, so we'll have to run through this quickly. Ooh, you've missed the entire orientation course!"

"WAIT wait. Wait," said Rodney. "Ginge, you're going back? As in, to Earth? How? And: are you crazy? It's Heaven up here...HEAVEN!" He squished my face between his chocolate-brown paws. He was puffed up bigger than the stuffed llama toy behind him. I had to calm him down, but before I could do anything, the bobtail nosed him aside.

"Not a lot of cats get to go back, which is why it's reeeally important he catches the next star down."

"Star?" we said together.

"Yes, you'll get there on a falling star. You'll have until Christmas Day's snowfall to help this kitten off the street and into his human's home."

"Christmas Day's snowfall? I don't know what day it is today!"

"You'll feel Christmas in your bones, just like you did when you were alive." She reached into the laundry at our feet and pulled out a toy cat with her teeth. The toy stood before me —white, except for a patch of gray on his head and a bigger blotch on his back, making his tail gray, too.

"Hey—I just met him yesterday decorating at Cleanwhisker. He's down already?"

"Time's funny up here," she said, waving a paw. "He'll be this size when you meet him. He needs to get to a girl named Nikki. Ughgh, oh, I wish I could at least give you the safety course. Listen, Gingersnap, while you're down there, you can't be hurt and you can't die, but you can be discouraged, and sometimes that's worse. Oh, and here." She began licking her paw pad. Her collar began to glow. Her mouth twisted in a funny way and she licked her paw down to her elbow three times. Then—*Whup! Whup! Whup!*—she swiped her sticky arm on me!

"Heyheyhey!" I yelled.

Rodney's eyes grew huge.

"Ginge! She gave you new stripes!"

I looked down. I could see one new stripe across my forelegs and another across my chest, breaking up my white blaze. Was the other one on my face?!

"Sorry," said the bobtail. "But I had to give you your miracles before you go. Three per assignment."

"Miracles!"

"Yeah, just little ones. They're a drop of—you know—the STUFF, Heaven's power. But you don't have to use them all up each assignment, and you're only supposed to use them for emergencies, and only to help in your mission." She patted the toy kitten. "No making snackies rain from the sky just 'cuz."

"Um," said Rodney, head twitching back and forth. "Are we moving?"

I jumped to the end of the laundry clearing and looked over the edge. The top of our laundry pile seemed to be stretching! The forest we'd come from looked a little like crumpled green Christmas wrapping, and was getting smaller every second. My claws shot out to keep me anchored to the ground. Good thing I didn't mind heights!

"We have to meet the star when it arrives," said the bobtail. "It won't come down to us!"

Rodney came over and joined me. "Hey, I can see my condo from here!" He pointed with his paw.

"Be careful!" said the bobtail.

A few minutes later, the stars around us stopped. In the distance, something glowing was heading our way. I stood up, then jumped back into a crouch. The moon seemed right on top of us, close enough to lick.

I slunk to the bobtail's side. "What else do I need to know?"

"Um...pay attention to your dreams, you could get messages in them. Or you might not! Oh, and if you see other angels, you'll be able to talk with them, even if they're human or a dog or whatever."

The glowing thing was getting bigger. Now I could see what it was: a weird-shaped wagon, with two huge front wheels like cages. A giant star rolled around in the middle of each wheel as it drove closer.

It rolled to a stop at our laundry pile. Someone—a human—stood up in the back. He smiled at me.

The bobtail spun around in a circle. "Oooh! I know I'm forgetting to tell you something! I guess if you need to know anything else, you'll get it in a dream!"

The man leaned over and opened a red door into the funny wagon.

"All aboard!" he said. When I stepped forward, he smiled at me. "Well, ain't you a handsome fella."

I like him already. Purring, I trotted into the red wagon-thing.

"Anyone else, darlin'?" he asked the bobtail.

"No, sir," she said.

"How 'bout him?" he lifted his chin at Rodney.

Rodney dove behind the bobtail. "Nuh-uh! Not me!"

The man chuckled, but nicely. "All right. Then we best be off." He shut the door. We were the only two standing in the wagon-thing, which was shiny and red inside. It reminded me of the backseat of a car, but with the seats and the back end missing. I prowled the bottom of the wagon-thing, looking for a good spot to curl up, but I got the horrible feeling that no matter where I settled down, I'd fall out the back once we got going.

"There's a seat up here for you, buddy," said the man. He pulled open the mouth to a fabric pouch, higher up. He let it go, and it stayed open. I dropped into a crouch, judging the distance, then leapt inside. I readjusted myself so my bottom was inside the pouch and my top was above it.

Now this was nice! There was a place for my paws to rest on the front lip of the wagon-thing, and I could see where we were going.

From up here, I could see the bobtail milling around in worry, and Rodney looking up at me.

"Good luck!" said the bobtail.

"Bye, Gingersnap! We'll miss you!" said Rodney.

"We'll be back up by Christmas," said the man. He touched my shoulder. "Everything good? You ready?"

I nodded.

"All right. Chariot, go!"

WHING! The wagon-thing—chariot—shot out in front of the moon.

I dug my claws into the wooden lip of the chariot.

"Quite a ride, ain't it?" the man asked me.

I nodded, but didn't look at him; I was too busy looking around. The view while flying was optimal; you could see most all the Earth in one glance, though of course you couldn't see any prey! But if something big was going on, you'd be the first to know!

"Name's Dwight," said the man. He had a brown beard and moustache, a hat, and big square fingers. "What's yours, kitty?"

"Gingersnap," I said.

"Good to meet ya." He offered me his hand. I leaned forward and gave it a sniff.

He laughed. "Sorry! I was more of a dog person on Earth, but they told me this mission could only be done by a cat. Is there a better way to greet a cat?"

"Wait," I said. "You know about my mission?"

"It's the same one," he said. "Same one I'm on," he added.

The wind whistled around us, but I barely felt the chill. Dwight pulled his green windbreaker tighter around him. "I'll be working the human side of the equation. Maybe we're supposed to meet up while we're down there, exchange notes."

"I might get dreams that tell me what to do."

"Whoa, yeah! Follow those before you listen to the schemin' of an angel!" He winked.

"But...I'd like to meet up. If we can?" Suddenly I felt like a squirrel-brain. I had no idea what I was doing! I should be in the bobtail's orientation class, not driving to Earth with a human stranger!

"Sure we can!" said Dwight. "Listen, I used to be like you. No clue *what* I was doin'!" He swiped his hands out in front of him, reminding me of my Damien. "Actually, I still am like you! Once you're down there, you gotta keep focus on your person—or cat, in your case—and wing it!"

I wrinkled my nose. "Wing it? Like a bird?"

The glow of the Earth was getting closer. He laughed. "Sorry. That's a human saying. I mean...you take it a step at a time. Maybe one day you get the feeling to go someplace. You don't know why, but you do it. And after you get there, more often than not, you get another idea, then do that. Before you know it"—he did that human snappy-noise thing with his fingers—"you've done your mission."

I waved my tail. "My mother taught us something like that—to check all the hunting spots in your territory, even if they were empty yesterday, since you'll never know what you'll find."

"Yeah," he said, rubbing his beard with his hand. "I guess it's a little like that. We humans call it faith. You know? To get somewhere, you only gotta see as far as the next step. One step's enough."

"Yeah," I said, watching some roofs come into view. "I can do that. One step's enough."

The nervousness of coming back to Earth wound around my excitement of doing something that mattered. Would I be a good angel? Could I help my street kitten?

But Dwight's advice helped keep my excitement and my fear from fighting.

One step's enough. That's all I need to see.

CHAPTER SEVEN

The red chariot touched down in the middle of a park. It was nighttime, but the park was lit by those strange orangey stick-light-trees that poked out of the sidewalks like too-long hooked claws. There weren't as many trees as I would have liked, and we were awfully close to one of those strange chair-building-toy-places human children liked to climb on and jump off of and slide down. I thought of them as "kiddie condos."

"I guess this is where you get off, Mr. Gingersnap," said Dwight.

I pedaled my back feet until I was out of the bag, then jumped onto the ground.

The moment my paws hit the ground, I knew things had changed. In Heaven, remember, you could feel things only a little. But the gray ground here felt hard and cold against my toepads. Had Heaven turned me into a tenderfoot?!

I flexed my claws, scenting the crisp air. Wow! The smell of pet dogs and their humans was distinct, wafting over the hard roads humans had made over the dirt hills of the park. But I was used to the smell of grass.

"Dwight?" I said. "Where's all the grass?"

"I think we're in Texas," he said.

"Is that a Housing?"

"Nah, it's a state! In the desert, or at least, part of it is. Hard to grow grass in the desert," he explained. "Not enough moisture."

"Moisture?"

"Yeah, you know, like rain or snow."

My tail swished. I was supposed to be done with my mission before Christmas Day's snowfall. Could it snow here?

The chariot began to lift. I jumped around, tail puffed. The stars in the wheels shone bright, brighter, began to whirr.

"Be careful out there!" called Dwight. "Don't get down-hearted. And who knows? I might be seeing ya soon! WHOA!" He said this last word just before the chariot disappeared into an orange streak blurring across the purple night sky. I followed the motion, fast as a sparrow's flight.

The wind whistled and my ears folded to keep the chill out. There might not have been any snow here in the park in Texas, but the wind was cold! I hadn't ever been cold in Heaven.

I ran up the slide for human children and crouched at the end of a tunnel with round windows. The wind whistled at the slide's mouth. I had no idea where my mission kitten was, my fellow angel was gone, and I'd forgotten how awful it felt being cold. Heaven and my Lord and all my friends felt very far away, their love a faded memory.

Why did I ever think it would be a good idea to come back to the streets?

CHAPTER EIGHT

"Hey. HEEY!"

I sprung awake. Hard orange walls surrounded me—nothing outside the round window looked like cat Housing. And facing me was a snarling black cat with a chipped fang. He was blocking my exit. My claws tried to dig in, but the floor of this place had many little holes in it.

"What?" I said.

He growled. "These are my digs! There ain't enough food 'round here for sharin'!"

"Oh! Um..." That's right. My mother had taught me if you could find land with enough prey, a few cats could share on it. But if times were tough, forget it!

"I'm new here. I just needed a place out of the wind for the ni—"

"Sure you did! I know a takeover when I see one!"

I got to my feet, bristling my fur so I looked like I filled the tunnel. He yowled at me again, but I'd already seen him flinch. I was big and strong from Heaven. He wasn't going to fight me if he could avoid it.

"I'm not interested in your turf. But if you want me to leave, better move aside, bud."

He growled in the back of his throat, but backed away. I could see cold daylight behind him, broken up by the hard shapes of the kiddie condo. I zipped past him, leapt down onto the rubbery ground beneath the condo, then turned around at the sound of his heavy body landing on something above me. He glared down at me from a purple box thing with spinning wheels facing out. "Get outta here!"

My whiskers twitched, ready to snarl back. But then a quiet feeling came over me, smoothing my fur. It was like being petted by a warm, invisible hand. I didn't feel like snarling anymore.

"What's your name?" I asked him. I hadn't planned on saying it, but out the words popped.

Now he looked surprised. His fur smoothed. He sat down, laying his tail over his front paws. "I'm Shade."

"Gingersnap," I said, bumping my tail against my chest. "Nice to meet you."

He frowned at me, but his scent on the air was confused, not angry.

"Shade, have you seen any kittens outside your territory? Well, guess I should say kits. They're older than newborns."

"Maybe," he said. "Why?"

"I'm looking for one—white, with a gray blotch on his head and back, and a gray tail. It's important."

He stared off into the trees. I thought of my miracles. Was now the time to use one? Maybe he'd help me if I promised him food...

"He your housemate?" Shade asked.

I looked at him, surprised. If he had ever lived with humans, it didn't show anymore.

"No," I said. "Did you have a housemate before?"

"Almost. Her name was Pepperoni," he said. "Her humans called me Olive. I didn't go inside the house, though. But Pepperoni was my wall-friend, 'til another tom took over her block. I like it here, though." His ear flicked in the wind. "Listen, uh, sorry 'bout earlier. I haven't seen a kit like that in my territory. You know what he smells like?"

The toy kitten hadn't had any scent—or at least, not one strong enough for me to remember on Earth. I shook my head no.

"Well, if I was a kit just starting out, I know the spot I'd try to stake out."

He slid his front paws down the front of the purple box, then jumped off it to land on the spongey ground. He curled the tip of his tail. "Come on. I'll point you in the right direction."

A *churr* escaped me. All this because I'd asked his name?

"Thanks for the help," I said.

I trotted to Shade's side and we set out opposite the rising sun. From time to time the breeze blew, but it moved about as fast as the breath from a snoring human, so I couldn't feel it through my fur. He walked us parallel to the dog-smelling path, close to bushes we could escape to.

"Do dogs come here often?"

"Every day," he said. "But with the cold weather coming, most the humans wait 'til the sun's up to walk 'em. Think it's warmer, though how they get on without proper coats, that's a curiosity I haven't answered yet."

"Some of those yarn pelts they wear are pretty warm. Some even warm themselves," I said, thinking of Marie's electric blanket.

"Where'd you come from, anyway?" he said. "You're big and clean like an Indoor cat, but I can't smell any human on you. I can't even smell where you came from! And..." He went quiet.

You didn't run back there, I finished for him.

He shook the words off his tongue and said something different. "It's like you flew in on wings!" he said.

I swallowed a chuckle. *If only you knew!*

"I've lived on both sides of doors," I said. Was I supposed to tell him I was an angel?

"Which do you like better?"

"Indoors," I said. "But only with the right humans."

"But Indoors, you lose so much territory! You can't come and go! Forget any Midnight Rallies! And you forget how to hunt!"

Sure hope I haven't forgot that!

"There's trade-offs either way," I said, pausing as he sharpened his claws on a wooden signpost. "I was hungry on the street a lot.

42

And lonely. My old territory wasn't so hot, though—definitely not as nice as what you have here. Do you manage the whole park?"

His chin lifted and his chest puffed. "Sure do!" Then his tail fell a little. "But only since the summer. Last tom disappeared, nobody's seen him since."

"Humans?" I'd been picked up by them. That's how I got to the shelter, and eventually to the Romanos. What it'd looked like to my fellow alley cats, I hadn't considered 'til now.

"Maybe," he said. "I hope. There's rumor a coyote—that's a wild-type dog—made it here deep in the city, but years ago the humans kept dropping their, you know, *personal* dogs off wherever."

"What?!"

"Some of 'em got picked up again by other humans, but others had to become alley dogs..." He flicked a whisker in disgust. "You can imagine how that turned out, poor chumps. One night, getting all the kibble they can eat and a warm crate, the next, gotta feed themselves with their own claws and jaws... But a very few of 'em remembered they're wolves at heart. They turned *mean*." Shade's hackles bristled with a chill that had nothing to do with the wind. "If you're ever cornered by one of them, you'd better hope a tree's nearby and claw your way to the tippy top."

All the dogs I'd watched from my window had been barky pushovers. Could there still be off-leash dogs out there who thought they were wolves? Things on the street had changed since I was a kit.

Shade paused to spray a bush. It faced a black plain with white lines on it. From vet visits, I remembered looking out the window and seeing many human growl-machines loafed between those lines, but right now the plains were empty.

"It's quiet back here, but if you turn towards your weak paw, you'll hit the main road. Cross it, then keep going 'til you smell the dumpster farm. There's a mess of them, and rats to go with 'em. Head thataway. If he ain't there, I don't know where he'd be.

"This is the edge of my digs," said Shade. "If I go past the boom -machine ground, I'll tick off Queen Chalky across the street, and we've been good neighbors for a while."

"Got it," I said. "Thanks for everything, Shade. If you ever want to live Indoors—"

"No, not me, tom! Living with humans ain't my scene. But I appreciate the kind whisker behind your offer." He slow blinked at me. "Good luck finding your kit."

Shade left me, melting into the shadows beneath a trash bin, disappearing after our goodbye.

I turned towards my off paw, smelling machine juice in the distance, hearing the roar of the human death-machines in the distance. If my kit wasn't at the dumpster zone, I didn't know where to look for him next.

"One step's enough," I murmured.

I set off for the main road.

CHAPTER NINE

Wheel machine fumes had long since soaked into the black-tar road and the bushes next to it. So while only one or two machines rumbled past, I knew there'd be a river of them soon enough.

Probably when the sun is higher.

But I hoped to be far away from the busy roads before then. The machines usually traveled in straight lines between the yellow marks on the tar, but once, when I was an alley cat, one of them had gotten hungry and had jumped for me, crossing the marks. If I hadn't thrown myself out of the way in time, I would have died!

I could hear the growl of its engine like it had just happened. I dropped my head to clean my chest, until the trembling stopped.

Come on, Gingersnap. Those machines can't hurt you now.

I took a deep breath, double, then triple-checked the road was clear, then hurried across. At the safe white path on the other side of the tar road, I stopped to pick a pebble from out between my paw pads. Then I sniffed the air. No dumpster smell yet, or restaurant smell, either. I padded forward.

When I was a kit, the mouthwatering salty smell of fries had called me to a dumpster back behind a human food place. I was normally a good ratter, but behind this joint, the rodents were extra wily. I wound up keeping it in my territory, though, when I realized how good the uneaten human food was—especially the fries, but also the buns and milkshakes. I was at least big enough to chase the rats off and eat the lion's share.

And if this dumpster spot was new enough that nobody had claimed it, word would definitely get out to the younger, less-established kits and queens. I just had to sniff it out, first.

The road parallel to the white walk was quiet. On my weak paw's side, cinder block walls had gone up around giant human boxes they liked to go in. Buildings. That was the word. My vet had been in one—shudder—but before you got to the vet there were smaller boxes with weird rodents and unopened cans of food. Why humans would hoard them together was beyond me. And why they never brought home a rodent for me, well…I used to think it was rude, but since being in Heaven I'd learned about Fancy Rat Housing and the Hamster Underground…So some of them had been pets, and, being a pet myself, I knew I'd feel betrayed if Marie or anyone ever tried to feed me to a bigger pet!

I scented a dog nearby. Dog with a human. I bunched myself up then leaped onto the top of the wall to continue my walk.

There he was—a dumb golden retriever on a leash held by a man, heading my way. But even if the man reached above his head, he wouldn't be able to reach me on the high wall. I decided to pretend they weren't there.

But of course, the dog couldn't let that happen. As soon as they were within noseshot, the dog started up.

"Dad! Dad, look! Is it Nemo?"

The man tugged on the leash. "Down, Jules, easy!"

I ignored him and hurried along.

The sun was finally visible in the sky, but at this time of year, it didn't warm my back; the cold air was too strong for it, unless you were Indoors. Ah, nothing like curling up Indoors inside a square of sunshine. Why, once my alley kit tried that, he'd be an Indoors cat for life!

Then I arrived at the next crossing on the wall and my happy sunshine feelings disappeared. My fur prickled at the scene beneath me. The machines were screaming through the black tar road, three abreast. It'd be impossible to cross! It was so noisy that I didn't even want to drop back onto the ground.

I tucked my tail beneath me.

Gingersnap! Crossing a road is so easy, even a dog can do it!

The dog! Dogs get walked all the time, and they don't get hit— not when they're with a human!

I turned around on the wall and raced back. I caught up with them.

"Dog! Excuse me, dog! What's your name?"

The man tried to keep walking, but the dog whipped around and stuck his paws against the wall. "Hello again! I'm Jules! You look like my cat friend Nemo! But you smell like a cloud! Are you new here? Do you need a place to stay? Do you have a—"

My tail curled. "Your housemate is a cat?"

"Sure is!" The dog said it like it was normal. "He's the best! Do you have a Forever Home?"

"Uh—I'm not looking. But I do have a question for you!"

His face lit up. "Yeah?"

"How do you and your master cross the street without getting hurt by the machines?"

"Oh, you mean the cars? That's easy. If you push the round shiny on the yellow poles, it'll make the birds chirp and you can cross faster."

"What?!" *He's nuts!*

"Yeah, Dad and I do it all the time."

My tail swished behind me. Birds? In poles? That stop the car-machines?

But I had nothing else to try.

I made myself purr. "Thanks, Jules! That's just...what I needed."

His golden face spread into a huge smile. It even warmed my heart, though Heaven knew I'd spent a lot of my time as a street kit hiding from dogs. But if his friend was a cat, then maybe he wasn't so bad. For a dog.

"You're welcome!" he said. "Don't get squashed!"

I shuddered. "I won't!"

"Byeeee!" said the dog, his master hauling on the leash.

So there's such a thing as a friendly dog. Who knew?

I turned back the way I came, picked up the pace, dying to know if the dog's trick would work. Yellow pole birds! Indeed!

* * *

Back at the river road, the cars rolled by, denser than ever. I frowned down at the pole from the wall. From here, I couldn't see the shiny. Maybe this was the wrong angle.

I leaned over the wall and jumped onto the safe path. I walked up to the yellow pole and began circling it. From here, I could see two shinies—one facing the road I wanted to cross, and one facing the road on my cleaning paw's side, the one I was traveling parallel to.

I jumped and smacked the one facing the direction I wanted to go with my paw. At first, nothing happened. I turned in a circle, *mrr*ing to myself. The monster cars roared on.

Then, to my surprise, a loud bird began to chirp, easily heard over the cars. I looked around, but couldn't see it. But I could *hear* it—chirping to a second bird in the yellow pole across the road on my cleaning paw's side.

The dog was right!

I fixed my eyes on that pole, waiting to see the bird.

CHIRP!

CHIRP.

CHIRP!

CHIRP.

My ears spun, listening to them chirp back and forth. Then, a car rolled up towards the two poles where the birds were chirping. But as it approached the pole-birds, it stopped, grumbling to itself.

A few seconds later, the chirping stopped, and the machine went forward.

My tail wagged. *Well, I'll be a sphinx's brush!* The cars *did* stop for the invisible birds.

I circled to the other side of the pole and smacked the other shiny. Almost immediately, the chirping began, but this time my pole bird was calling to the one in the direction I needed to go in. And all the rows of cars had stopped, and were grumbling in place. I ran forward, keeping my nose pointed straight at the yellow pole opposite my crossing. I flung myself onto the safe white road on the other side, tail straight up. *Ha. Take that, rumbly monsters!*

I sneezed out their awful smell and kept heading up my path, keeping my nose alert for any dumpster smells.

CHAPTER TEN

I had to cross two more roads before I began smelling the restaurant's dumpsters, but the dog's trick worked both times. I was glad he had a Forever Home and a good cat taking care of him. I was even sorry I called him dumb.

I turned off the safe path and into the shadowy parts behind more human boxes. My nose brought me scents that reminded me of a special kind of fry they used to throw out in my dumpster... Pungent, buttery, but minus the potato smell here.

I followed the smell back to a dark yard behind a human box that smelled like spaghetti night at our house. The dark yard was walled in except for a metal gate that was cracked open. It was like a box with no top and street for the bottom. Up this close tomatoes and spoiling beef joined the pungent butter on the air.

Leaning around the gate let me safely see the green dumpster sitting just inside the gate. I sniffed again, checking for rats. None here—yet. It'd only be a matter of time, though, before they moved in on this hot spot.

This place must be REALLY new if the rats haven't arrived yet.

The corners of the walls had been marked by several different cats and at least one raccoon, with none of the scents sticking out in particular. It was one big pileup as everyone raced to claim the dumpster, and no one had chased away the others for good.

I minced inside the gate, whiskers tingling as they brushed the metal edge. I stalked the gap in between the dumpster and the walls. If a cat was hiding back here, it'd be tough to smell him over the spaghetti-night odors. The dumpster threw a deep shadow back in the corner.

Klitterklitterklitter!

My fur exploded and I darted out the gate. After a second to catch my breath, I realized what I'd heard sounded familiar... not an animal, not a human...but I couldn't place the sound! What could it be?

The sun was rising higher. More cats could be here soon. I didn't like the thought of being trapped in that corner if they came, but I couldn't get that rattling out of my head. I growled at myself and padded back in.

Klitterclatter, went the shadow. But this time I wasn't so keyed up. I stuck around and really *looked* at the shadow. It was a cage

—like my carrier, but without the plastic sides. And inside was a kit, shaking.

"Hello?" I said. I could only make out his shadow, even his scent was muddled.

"Back off! Back! Off!"

He spat at me, tiny needle teeth gleaming in the shadow.

"What happened?" I asked.

"It's my can! My can! But now I can't get out!"

Can?

I circled the cage, out of reach of his arm, trying to claw me. Sure enough, at the back of the cage was a can. A quick sniff—tuna, crusted dry on metal bars. Damien had set traps like this—for "darn varmints", he called them. I think he caught something once, but I'd been sleeping when it happened and only heard about it after he and Gina had come back, smiling and smelling like Outdoor wood and fresh air.

But now this kit had gotten himself stuck in one and I didn't know what kind of human had set it or where he might take the kit when he came back.

I checked over my shoulder at the gate. I didn't know what would be worse—alley cats showing up, or a human.

All the while, the kit was hollering at me. "You puffy dogface! If I wasn't in here, I'd claw you to rat tails! Come over here so I can cut you. This dumpster's MINE!"

All this noise would bring a human by any second now!

"Hush!" I hissed.

He shrunk into a ball. *Big talk, little claws*, that's what my mother used to say about us kittens.

"I don't want your dumpster. I'm trying to find someone."

"Yeah?" he said. "Who is it?"

"A kit—about your age, I reckon—white, with gray patches on his head, back and tail."

"Got a name?"

"No," I said. "I just got here. But I have to find him."

"Well, if you leave me in here, you're making a big mistake. I know all the kits around here!" I could hear the way he puffed out his chest out as he spoke.

I studied him, but still couldn't make out much more than a dark shape. Too dim. On the one paw, he'd spent almost all the time I'd known him cursing and swiping at me with his claws. But on the other paw, Shade and Jules had been helpful, and I hadn't exactly liked them at first sniff, either.

If this kit *did* know everybody—and he could be lying, I knew—it'd help me with my mission. And that's what I was down here for, wasn't it?

My tail wagged as I thought. But the kitten sat quiet, not even trembling.

I guess it's good I can't see him. Don't want any sad kitten eyes making my decision for me.

"This angel stuff is hard," I muttered.

"What?"

"Nothing. Listen, you get in the back and stay still. I need some light so I can look at the latch."

He sat back by the upset tuna can and I got behind him. I bowed my head against the prickly cage and pushed forward.

Squeak! Snakkasnakka! The cage's bottom scraped against the ground. I got it closer to the gate, but had to stop to get it around the tight corner. We were still in shadow. I needed light!

I was checking out a better angle to push at when I heard the unmistakable *click* of a door opening. Me and the kit froze.

My ears tracked the whistling of a human—and then a *thump-clang*. Garbage bags were raining down into the dumpster! How long before one hit me?

I shot back into the dark corner.

"HEEEY! Don't leave me!" cried the kit.

"We got one!" said the human from the other side of the wall. A woman. I flattened my ears even more, trying to become one with the ground. The kit's shadow was looking all around.

"Off to the shelter with you, mess maker!" The human footsteps beat the ground, and then the gate was pushing open. A woman wearing black shoes with thick soles and black pants stepped inside. I was frozen in place, unable to swipe at her or even call out.

On sight of her, the kitten wailed. Poor, stupid kit, he's just bringing her closer!

The woman scanned the shadows.

I closed my eyes tight.

"Aha!" She pointed at the cage. I peeked one eye open, but her legs blocked my view. The cage was shaking again, *klitter-klitter-klitter!* There was no way for him to escape!

The kitten needed a miracle to get out of there, and I was carrying three of them.

He can't help me if he's not safe and free. I need to use my miracle NOW!

The stripe across my legs squeezed against me like a warm hug and then left me feeling light, just for a second. I leaned to one side, excited to see what would happen to her or the cage.

But the woman bent down, blocking my view. The cage was still shaking.

The kit was still inside. The latches or whatever hadn't popped open and the trap was still closed. Panic fluttered into my heart. Did I just waste my first miracle?

The kit cried again, louder than ever. "I'm scared! I don't like this. I want my mama!"

There was a pause. And then: "Awww!"

My ears perked. The woman's voice was sweet now, the way Gina used to talk to me. "Poor little guy!"

"*Maaa,*" whimpered the kit.

"It's okay, sweetie! It's all right! I know you're not the one making all this mess at night! You're too small to make any trouble, aren't you?"

"*Maaa,*" said the kit.

"That's right!" she nodded her head. "Only a mean ol' raccoon could lift the lid. You just got stuck in here by accident, didn't you, kitty?"

"*Maaa.*"

"OK, then." Her voice dropped to a whisper. "I won't tell Mr. Baker if you don't," she said to the kit.

I heard more cage noises. Then:

"There you go! That's better! C'mon! Good boy!"

I still couldn't see past the woman's back. But then the woman stood, cage dangling in her hand. It was empty.

"Don't come back, now! If you do, I'll have to take you to the shelter!" She shook her finger at the air. Then she left the dumpster box, closing the gate behind her. At last, I became unfrozen.

What happened?!

After I heard the door click shut, I leaped to the top of the wall. Decent sightlines, except where the human-boxes blocked the view. I scented the air, but the wind gusted and all I got was car fumes and butter.

"Kit?" I said. I turned around. "Kit?"

"*Mew.*"

It was the tiniest squeak, more mouse than feline, but my ear found its source: between a little bush with purple flowers, part of a weird little island-box of plants next to the car lines. I leaped down and scooted into the bush with him.

"You okay, kit?"

He was trembling again. I gave his ears a good wash, but he was still twitchy as a bird. "You're all right now."

I thought back over today. "What's your name?" I asked.

He didn't answer.

"I'm Gingersnap."

Still nothing. I licked the fur bristling on his back, but it only popped back up again. I touched his face with my paw. I was an angel now and I wanted to be kind, but it was hard to resist batting him in the nose when we were surrounded by car lines and no shiny things in sight to stop them. Not to mention other humans with traps, maybe ones who were miracle-proof.

"Hey. Wake up," I said to him with a voice much gentler than I normally could have used. "You said you'd help me find that other kit. If he's in a cage, we have to save him. Can you get your fur smooth for me? We can't go if you're puffed like a sparrow dressed for winter." The picture of him toddling behind me like a big cloud of fuzzy gray made me chuckle. "At least, I'm not going to walk around with you looking so hilarious."

He gave me an indignant look, then swooped around to groom his back. I leaned over to flatten the hard-to-reach spot behind his head. When he was finished, he threw out his chest again, frowning face so serious I could have laughed.

"Ready to come out?" I said.

He hopped out of the bush onto the black road. I just about fell over.

"You're my kit!" I said. "I know you!"

58

In the full sunlight I could see him tip to tail. It wasn't just that he was a white cat with the correct number of gray patches—I recognized him from decorating the tree at Cleanwhisker.

"What?!" He took a step back, gawking at me like I was crazy.

"I'm supposed to find you and...and get you to Nikki! This is great!"

"Huh?!"

I opened my mouth to answer, but instead, the kit bolted. I sat for a second watching his gray tail grow smaller as he got further away from me. My angelic patience deserted me. I took off after him.

"HEY!" I yowled. "I'm trying to help you! Stop!" The little hairball!

The tar road was warm under my paws. I was almost on him when he veered off, turning the corner out of sight behind a building.

"Stop, stop!" I called.

I turned the corner and my anger turned to fear. He was heading towards a car that was zooming in front of the building, both moving too fast to stop.

The monster screeched.

The kit looked up from checking behind his shoulder at me and saw the monster bearing down on him. He froze.

NO!

Everything slowed down. I saw individual strands of his pelt bend with the wind, I saw tar grit being thrown out by the machine's giant smelly wheels in an arc, slow and smooth as a dangling string.

And yet I never stopped running at full speed. I blinked and was right on top of the kit, the world still moving slowly, impossibly slowly. I heard somehow the sound of the little kit taking a deep breath. The car continued forward, crawling towards us, its metal mouth brushing my whiskers. But I grabbed the kit by the scruff with my teeth and ran, ran as fast as I could out of the way.

Woosh.

I looked around. Green surrounded us. My claws were dug into the wood of a leafy tree. And the kit was still hanging from my jaws, his blue eyes wide. Time had returned to normal.

"Hummina...hummina..." I thought I heard him say.

My legs were shaking too, so I gripped the thick tree branch extra hard with my claws, creeping back towards the trunk. Where the branch connected to the tree made a safe, wide cradle for us to sit in, so I finally set the kit down. We crouched together, tails around each other, trembling together.

After a few minutes, he finally spoke.

"You...saved my life."

I sighed. "Yeah. Just don't ask me how we got up this tree."

We both started laughing—out of relief, more than anything. When we were done, I licked the top of his head again.

"My mother named me Graypatch," said the kit, wrinkling his nose. "But I like 'Patch' better." Then he blinked up at me. "Now tell me your story. From the beginning."

CHAPTER ELEVEN

The kit—Patch—took the news of me being an angel pretty well —until he asked me what an angel was. Then it was a thousand questions, just like it is with any kit—was it weird being dead, did I have wings, were any of my siblings still alive, could I always use that super speed...I finally had to put a paw in his face and tell him to hush and that I couldn't tell him EVERYTHING about me. Besides, it seemed like every time I wanted to talk about my life in Heaven, the words wouldn't come, but would sit there peering over their backs at me.

Luckily, there are two things you can count on with any kit: first, they're always only a few minutes away from a nap. Second, they're always hungry.

So he stopped asking questions about me and started asking about lunch. I got a feeling this warm winter—well, warmer than I was used to, anyway—would confuse some birds. Luckily, I was right, finding some bird eggs in a nest on a lower branch.

"Here," I said after dropping it at Patch's paws.

"Oo! I love egg goop, thanks!" He lapped it all up before I could blink. I hadn't felt hungry anyways. Thinking back, I realized that the spaghetti-night smells at the kit's dumpster hadn't even made my tummy gurgle. My tail curled, wondering. *Maybe angels don't need to eat.*

Eggshell dry, my kit stretched, tongue lolling in a big yawn.

"Have a nap, kit. You've had a big morning."

"Thanks. Don't mind"—he yawned again, so wide I could see his molars—"if I do." He dropped off in the flick of a whisker.

I sniffed the branch he was on. Satisfied it was strong and safe, I kicked the empty eggshell out of the tree and climbed out to the edge of the limb to get a better look at things.

We had taken up residence in a big tree that was just one in a line of them that followed a hard white footpath in grass. All of them, including ours, seemed to have paper balls in them— Christmas decorations?

I could also hear cars faintly, but couldn't see them. I crossed to the opposite side of the tree. Over a wall was a fence around a big grass field, which was around a huge human building and a couple of kiddie condos. It'd only take us a couple minutes to get there.

Brrrrriiing! The building shrilled, making my ears flatten. Then hundreds of human children poured out of the building and scattered—though most of them were going to the far side of the building where I couldn't see them. I was thoroughly confused until I caught a glimpse of a macaroni-noodle yellow, big long machine leaving the building. I'd seen Gina off on the bus like that for years. Was this where it went? Was it "school"? Was this where Patch needed to be?

Soon, children were clumping down the white path beneath us. They wore backpacks just like my Gina did, chattering like mice. One boy passing under our tree pointed. He had a funny cap on, green.

"Hey! An eggshell!"

He looked up and I caught a glimpse of brown eyes. I darted back to the trunk.

"Look! A cat!" he said.

"Are you sure?" said a girl. "It could have been a Christmas decoration. They put teddy bears or something on one by my house."

"No, there was a cat. Here, I'll show you!"

I heard a backpack thud like it had been dropped, and some scrabbling at the base of the tree.

"I think that tree's too big to climb, JP. WAY too big."

"Yeah." I heard a sigh, and then I thought I heard his shoe clunk the trunk. "Wish I could, though."

The voice—JP—faded as he walked away. I peeped out, then ducked again when I saw him looking back. He held my eye for a second, then joined his chattering friends down the road.

The sun was going down. It was time for a nap of my own. I climbed back down the trunk to my kit. I peeled off the trunk as quietly as I could, thinking he'd still be asleep. Instead, he was a shock of fur glued in place, his eyes wide and fearful.

My tail jittered. "What's wrong?"

"Was that a human?" he asked, trying not to move his mouth.

"Sure," I said. "What's wrong with humans?"

"My mother told me to stay away from them."

"She did?" A hazy memory rose in the back of my head, of my mother gathering us kittens around, but too much time had been kicked up over her words, burying them.

"Why?" I asked.

"Humans will drown you. Or throw rocks that hurt. And they ride those big roaring things that can kill you! Or they'll take you away from your territory and you'll never come back!"

I wrinkled my whiskers. I'd heard some of the sadder ways cats made it to the Rainbow Bridge, and I could remember racing away from a noisy human more than once in my lifetime. And there were the cars. But I'd also met generations of pampered cats, raised or rescued by humans after a tough life Outdoors.

"Have any of those bad things ever happened to you?" I asked carefully.

His tail wagged. "Once. I was looking for some food by this human thing—it had boxes that slid out of the main box..." His ears flapped, looking unhappy.

Like a sock drawer, maybe. "Go on."

"Anyway, some little humans stuffed me in the box and shut me up. It really hurt! I couldn't breathe!" He was trembling again, so I went to his side and groomed him.

When he was calmer, I asked, "How did you make it out?"

He lowered his ears. "One of them pulled the box out a little to peep at me. I scratched him in the face as hard as I could, then ran away." He bared his fangs. "I don't like humans. Let's leave this tree tonight."

I looked around. Night was almost here. I didn't want to travel in a territory I didn't know in the dark.

"We can't," I said.

"What?!" he sharpened his claws. "Why not?"

"Because we're supposed to be here," I heard myself say. "And because you're meant to be more than an alley cat." The words coming out of my mouth were news to me! But as I said them I knew they were the truth. "A human needs your help."

"A human!" He clawed the bark again. "Get somebody else to do it!"

"But..." I faltered. "But that's why I'm down here! You have to join up with this human."

"Sure—a little kit like me would be a perfect toy for some human to pull on...or chase...or throw!"

"Not all humans are like that," I said. "I grew up an alley cat, like you," I said. "And one day, humans *did* take me from my territory."

He sat up, tail straight. "They did?"

"Mmhmm."

"What happened then?"

"I went into a place they call a 'shelter.' A shelter is Indoors. Have you ever been Indoors before?"

He shook his head.

"Well, Indoors is different. But hard to explain. Anyway, I lived in a cage for a while. See, I was lots older than you when I was taken away. Most humans like to raise cats from when they're kittens. But not all. My Damien—" I shook my head. "When I saw him I knew he was my human. He didn't know it, though, 'til I grabbed him passing by on the way out." I held out my paw, fingers open, claws spread. My claws had snagged on his black sweater and our eyes had met. In them I saw what my heart already knew: we would make a great team, he and I. Then he had to have me.

"Then what happened?"

"He made pen marks on some papers, and then he took me home. I lived Indoors from then on, but I was never cold, always fed and..." My tail looped, trying to word this right "...I got to be a part of a family again."

"But...they're...so different!"

"Well, yeah. They have their own ways. But they're funny sometimes—like how they trip on things in the dark—"

"They DO that? But...can't they see?"

I chuckled. "Nope! They've got night blindness, compared to you and me. And have you ever seen one jump?"

"No."

I guffawed. "When they jump, they barely clear the floor. It's like this—" I did a pathetic hop, barely a paw's-width off the ground. Patch rolled on this back, mute with laughter.

"But they're not just funny, Patch. They take care of you. They rub the itchy spot right between your shoulders whenever you need it. They brush you so you don't cough up so many hairballs. And they talk to you in a special voice, so you never feel lonely. They're not perfect, but they can be...they can become a part of you."

He hid his face in his tail. "Hm..."

"So can we stay in this tree tonight?" I asked.

"You promise humans won't come take us in the night?"

"I promise. Besides"—I waved my tail at the darkened sky—"they can't see in the dark, remember?"

Just then, lights wrapped around the tree trunk flickered on, *BLINK!*

We both jumped, and then the kitten glared at me.

"Heh," I said, grinning. "Christmas lights."

He laid his chin on his paws. "I'm still not helping no human," he said.

What a wrinkle!

"It's your choice," I said, and licked his head once more. I stayed up a while after the kit started snoring. I looked into the lights and prayed. *If this kit has to live with humans, Lord, he has to get over his fear of them. Your birthday will be here soon. Please help me get Patch ready. Amen.*

I wrapped my tail around my nose and fell asleep.

CHAPTER TWELVE

The next morning was as gray as Patch's tail and the wind cut through my pelt. Snow weather. I remembered it from my alley cat life on Earth. But it wouldn't snow until Christmas. I had 'til then to get Patch to his human.

"Eegh." Patch shivered next to me. "I've never been this cold before."

I looked him over. Short-haired—less than a year old. Not close to full grown yet. This definitely was his first winter.

"If you learn to live with humans," I said, "you'll never be this cold again."

His teeth chattered. "Really?"

I nodded. But then he frowned. "But I'll never go Outdoors again, will I?" His hackles bristled.

"No," I said. "But cars—those roaring monsters—don't come Indoors. Ever." Garages didn't count. They were too cold.

The mice-chatter of human children drifted upwards to our branch. Patch crouched low, ears following the footsteps below us.

Hmm. Talking isn't working.

"Hey, Patch. You hungry?"

The frown slipped off his face and he nodded eagerly.

"Watch this."

I made my way to a lower branch and waggled my head, trying to see better. It was that boy in the green cap walking alongside a girl in a pink puffy jacket. The girl pulled a purple bag on wheels that rumbled against the ground. No one else was around them. I began climbing down the trunk.

"What are you doing?!" Patch whispered.

"Stay there. Just watch." I said, and then I dropped down in front of the boy. I heard one last panicked *Nngle!* from the kit, then blocked him out as the boy and girl gasped in delight.

"You were right!" said the girl. Her eyes were bright through pink glasses.

"Toldja!" The boy knelt. "Heya, girl," he said to me.

It wasn't the first time a human had called me a girl. Heck, every time Gina brought home new friends at least one did it. I figured the mistake had something to do with their funny-shaped human noses, unable to fathom my proud tom scent—but that was just guessing.

The boy began scratching me behind the ears. A little hard, but I didn't smell dog on his hands. Maybe he didn't have pets. I turned to the side and he rubbed the length of my back instead. I purred.

"Aww," said the girl. She fumbled off a mitten—strawberry-milkshake scent puffed into the air, lotion, maybe?—and pulled a colorful rectangle out of her backpack pocket. While I studied the pink and white stars on it, it went *click*.

"Your parents let you have a phone?" asked the boy, still petting me.

"Only for emergencies," she said. She looked into her rectangle. "Aww. So cute."

The boy bit his lip. "Can you send it to me?"

"Sure!" said the girl. The rectangle made clicks as she poked it with her finger. I took a step towards the boy, giving him a good sniff over. No, no dogs or fancy rats or other cats. Clean. Had a faint smell of another place on him, though I couldn't say where...I hopped my front paws on his shoulder (which got a delighted giggle out of him) so I could get a better whiff of his backpack. Papers...old candy...pencil wood...

Tweet-tweet! Went the girl's phone. "Sent it. Aww, she likes you."

"The whiskers tickle!" said the boy.

...then the smell of bread hit me. *Aha. Found it.*

I pawed at the zipper on the boy's bag. "What's in your lunch?" I asked.

70

The girl clapped her hands. "Aw, listen to him talk! *Mao-mao!*" She echoed at me.

"Naaw, you don't want to come to school with me, girl," said the boy. He tried moving my paws but I moved away, butting my head into his hands.

"She likes you, JP!" said the girl. "And wants something in your backpack," she said as I raked my soft paws over the zipper, pretending to dig. The boy gently elbowed me aside, then pulled the zipper apart. I stuck my face in, sniffing around his binders and crinkled green hot fries wrappers.

Aha! There it was! I reached my paw in.

"What's she want?" asked the girl.

JP, the boy, pulled out the thing I was touching. It was another bag, blue and soft, with lumpy-looking yellow characters on it. I pawed its yellow zipper, looked at him, and gave my saddest mew.

"Awww!" said the girl.

The boy's voice turned soft. "You hungry, girl?"

I mewed again.

He unzipped the bag.

Score. Now I could smell tuna and mayonnaise with the bread. Just the thing for a growing kit. Purring, I plunged my head into his lunch bag and snatched the sandwich out, baggie and all. The baggie was sticky and bland in my mouth. I only had it by a corner; the rest dangled almost to the tops of my paws. I looked at them both. She was grinning behind her hands and he was trying not to laugh.

I sat down, still watching him. His mouth went up in a smile, and his eyes crinkled, but for a second I saw something different behind them. I couldn't tell if it was pain or hope.

He took the bottom end of the baggie with one hand. I let it go. The whole thing flopped over in his hand. I reached out with my paw and touched his hand. It was a little cold from the sunless day. Sometimes you needed somebody to do things for you, things you couldn't do yourself. I didn't know if he knew this. He was new to cats. Maybe he'd just pack up the sandwich and leave.

I looked up into his face again. My whiskers twitched as something passed between us.

You're on the right track. It sounded like someone whispering right in my ear. But before I could see who it was, the baggie was crinkling. I watched as the boy opened the sandwich. One sandwich turned into two breads, one topped chock full of tuna and mayonnaise and other good smells. The other bread had a green leaf on it, and a pale glaze of mayonnaise.

He folded the bread with the leaf in one hand so it turned into a half-sandwich. The tuna bread he offered to me.

"Here you go, girl," he said. I sniffed it over one last time, grabbed the side with my mouth, then turned and jumped up the tree. The tuna bread went with me.

"Whoa!" said the kit, skittering over his feet in surprise. I set the bread before him and he began snorfling it down. Footsteps pattered towards the base of the tree. I peered down the trunk. The children looked back up at me, mouths agape.

72

"She's not eating it!" said the girl.

"Someone is—you can hear it!" said the boy. "Wonder if she has a kitten." He said this with a puzzled frown, taking off his cap and running his hand through his sandy hair.

"You can have some of my lunch," said the girl. "Just not my Ding Dong."

He turned to her, face bright with a grin. "We'll see about that!"

I leaned back into the tree.

Zip, went his backpack. Then: "See you after school! Bye, kitty!"

While their footsteps went away, the kit stared at me. He had only licked the tuna off the top of the bread, leaving it bare.

"Was he talking to YOU?" he said.

"Sounded like it."

Patch sat back on his haunches and was quiet for a while.

In the meantime, I groomed the fur on my back smooth again. The boy's hands had left a not-unfamiliar hint of basketball rubber in my fur.

"Huh," the kit finally said.

"Were you watching?" I said.

"Yeah. Boy, he petted you rough!"

"At first some of them do. I don't think he's been raised with animals, by the smell of him. But you see he didn't pull on me. Or yell."

"No," the kit admitted, with only one suspicious flop of his tail. "Do you think he'll really come back?"

"He said he'd be back after school. Want to meet him then?"

"No!" He flattened his ears. Then: "He called you a girl."

"Well, someone will correct him later. Besides, it's not like it's a BAD thing to be called. How was the tuna?" I tilted my head at the bread.

"Tuna?" He licked his lips with a little purr. "Is that what that was?"

"Mmhmm. Humans buy it by the case. And this boy was happy to share."

"Yeah, but...How do you know this is my human?"

"It's not."

His fur puffed. "So I could be going to someone really mean!"

You're on the right track.

"No. I mean, it's a possibility. But I don't think so."

"But you don't *know*-know."

He'd set his lip in a frown. The hollows between his ribs showed when he breathed. That half-sandwich had been a feast. He hadn't been on Earth for a dozen weeks, but already he had the cynicism and doubt of an alley oldster. Things were hard down here. I'd forgotten.

"You angel cats must get fed and groomed lots by humans to love them, but some of us just have to get by. Why should I trust them? Humans took my mom away."

"What?" I said. "You didn't mention that!"

He nodded. "She went off to hunt and left us alone. When she didn't come back, I looked for her. A human was taking her away in a cage, putting her in a monster-car-thing-whatever. I wanted to go to her, but she told me to stay."

"I'm sorry," I said.

"Then it was just me and my brothers and sisters," he whispered. He looked at me. "Why would they do that? Why did humans take my mother?"

"They might not have known. Humans don't know everything."

His tail waved off my words. "We stayed together as long as we could, but there wasn't any territory that could feed us all. I haven't seen them since." Patch bowed his head.

I went to his side. He butted his head into my blaze. "How can anything be all right again?"

His warm breath sniffled into my soft fur. I wrapped my tail around him in the cold morning. It took me a while to sort through my thoughts.

"I've felt like that before," I said. "Before I was an angel, I was a pet cat, and before I was a pet cat, I was an alley cat, and before I was an alley cat, I was an alley kit, like you."

"Yeah?"

"Yeah. And I've felt like you're feeling when I was each of these things."

He lifted his head, eyes full of confusion. "Yeah?"

I nodded. "My mother wasn't taken away. But, like all mother cats, she left us. And that wasn't so bad, but when my siblings went off their own ways, that hurt. Even though I knew it was coming, knew it was the regular way of cats, it hurt. I stuck with my brother Russet for as long as he'd let me, but one night, he snuck off after a queen and never came back. I was left behind. And it hurt.

"And when I was picked up by humans—in a cage and put in a big dark car, like your mother—wow." My hind claws dug into the wood at the memory. "It felt like the world had broken apart under my feet. I was scared for a while that they were going to hurt me. But they didn't. Instead they just...kept me in the cage. Oh, no one was ever mean to me, and I got fed—but for a long time, nothing changed. That was scary too, but in a different way. I sat looking through the bars of my cage, watching humans walk away with a kitten in a cage—I was older by then —and I wondered if I'd ever get picked, and how long I'd live in the shelter if I never did."

"Then you got your family. D-d..."

"Damien. And his mate Marie, and their little baby, Gina, who could only talk and walk a little when I came into the picture. Those were happy times—and sometimes boring ones!" I chuckled. "But boring can be good, too. But at the end, I got real sick. I was an old cat! It was the way of things. But I hurt and I wanted to die, so I could feel better. But I knew if I died, I wouldn't be with my humans anymore. And I thought, 'how can anything be all right again?' And...well...you see me now." I lifted my tail. He batted at it with his paw. "I'm a healthy angel on Earth, and helping kits like you!"

"Will you ever see your family again? Your cat family, I mean?"

"Sure! Already met them up in Heaven. They'd been up there long before I got there, though. We had some good little get-togethers..." *And when I get back, maybe we should have some more...* "But, you know—well, I guess you don't know yet, you're so young...What I'm trying to say is, it's not just blood and mothers that make a family."

"It isn't?"

"No! It's the time you spend together and the things you go through. That all adds to the love that makes a family *feel* like family."

"Huh!" he said. "What about your human family? Will you see them again?"

"Absolutely! They're on their missions—living life—and now I'm on this one, with you. I guess what's important, kit, is that. You know as low as life gets sometimes, things get better."

"Really?" said the kitten.

"They really do," I said.

His eyelids lowered a little. Whether in deep thought or a kitten pre-drowse, I wasn't sure.

"Will you come down with me later to meet the children?" I said.

"Idunno," he said, wobbling forward. He lay down and pillowed his head on my paws. "Maybe."

Children's footsteps were passing by under our tree. He could sleep on it. He had all of school to decide.

While he slept, I leaned over and finished up the bread, purring to keep us both warm.

77

CHAPTER THIRTEEN

The school bell had rung minutes ago and many children had passed under our tree, but no sign of JP and his friend. When I wasn't carefully leaning my nose over the trunk to check for them, I was washing Patch. Sure, most humans fell for kittens his age like brown leaves in autumn, but I didn't want to leave anything to chance.

"Nygh!" went Patch as I scrubbed his cheek with my tongue. He jumped away. "I'm clean already, OK?"

"No rubbing your chin on the bark," I said. "Or I'll have to do it again."

He let out a pained sigh, flipping his tail against the tree. "Do you think they'll have food again? Those bugs you caught us didn't fill me up."

"I don't know," I said. Gina's lunch box always came home empty after school. I knew because I supervised Marie while she washed it. But children are like cats, every one a little particular. Maybe JP wasn't a big eater.

"I'm so hungry, I could eat a pine cone."

The boy smelled almost identical to the other boys, but when I smelled his hint-o-basketball whiff next to her strawberry milkshake-scented hand cream, well, I felt good about the odds. Then I saw the green cap.

"*Hsst!* It's them!" And only them. The parade of children hurrying home had thinned out until there were big gaps of silence between the sounds of bike wheels, footsteps, and voices.

JP and his friend came silently to the base of the tree. They both looked up.

"Here, kitty, kitty!"

I waited a dignified stretch of time between their calls and my reaction. In life, I'd only answered to my name when food dish noises were involved, and there was no point in breaking the habit now.

I turned to Patch.

"Ready to meet them?"

He bent his head, trying to see down the trunk. Every whisker was in place and the dark fur on the top of his head was soft and free of dirt and grit.

"You're sure it's safe?"

"Trust me. I know humans. These are good ones."

He gurgled in his throat, sounding unsure. "OK, Gingersnap."

"Then follow me. Tail first, you're not a squirrel." I set my claws into the bark and backed down the trunk. A gray tail tickling the back of my ear assured me Patch was following, even as I watched the ground over my shoulder, coming down tail-end first.

"She brought her kitten!" whispered the girl.

"Um...that's not a girl cat, Marta."

"It's not?"

I hopped off the tree.

"When he was climbing down I saw..."

I stretched quickly on the ground, then turned around to check on Patch's progress.

"Oh. Oh! Sorry, kitty," said the girl to me. I gave her a slow blink to tell her, *No problem.*

Patch stepped onto the sidewalk next to me. He took one look at the children then darted behind me.

"Aww, are you shy, boy? It's okay." The girl was doing a good job of talking quiet and not moving so much. The boy set his backpack on the ground and unzipped it. While he poked around in it, his pack rustled, and Patch peeked out to look.

I sniffed. Plastic.

The boy held up a bottle of water. "You got the dish?"

"Oh! Sure. Sorry." The girl dropped to one knee and pulled out her lunch bag, one that had a picture of a brown robot with big eyes. I wanted to go over and investigate, but when I leaned forward to go, Patch pressed tighter against me.

Unzipping her robot bag, the girl brought out an empty plastic container. She popped the lid off and I smelled old milk and blueberries. Maybe yogurt had been in there, but now JP was unscrewing the lid of the water bottle and pouring some water into the container. He filled it a ways, then they both scooched back, sitting on their bottoms.

"Come on," I said to Patch. "When's the last time you drank something? At the dumpster?"

"No! I had a little in a black tube when I came down earlier to use the dirt."

"From a sprinkler head? That's not enough. Come on." I stood and walked towards the water. Since he was still leaning against me, he almost fell flat on his face! But he turned his overbalance into the start of a gallop and beat me to the water. Keeping his eyes on the children, he began to drink. While he did that I sauntered up to the boy.

"Hey, fella." He patted my head again with a heavy hand and I turned so he'd get my side instead. "This your friend?"

"The patch on his back looks like a saddle," said the girl. "Giddyap!" She giggled.

Patch froze, throat working as he watched her.

Seeing him, she quieted. "It's okay," she crooned. She lowered her palm to his back, but he skittered sideways, looking at me. I purred to reassure him and he stayed still—but out of reach of her hand. Only when she put her hand back in her lap did he return to the water dish.

The boy sighed, scritching my shoulders. Aah.

Then, suddenly, he turned to his pack and began taking everything out. The hot fries package got stuffed in his windbreaker pocket along with his crumpled papers and tissues. He reached over for the girl's backpack, but she yanked it away, wheels burbling on the sidewalk. Patch startled, splashing water on himself before he tried hiding beneath me.

"What are you doing?" The girl's teeth flashed a little at the boy.

"If Nikki won't come to school, she'll never see the cats."

I mrred in excitement. Nikki!

"I have to bring them to her."

The girl's anger loosened from her face, turning confused.

"Nikki? Who's Nikki?"

"My sister." His jaw jutted out.

"Why haven't you talked about her before?"

"You gonna help, or what?"

"Help you do what? Empty your bag?"

"Yes! It's the only way. See?"

"So...you want me to carry your stuff in my bag so you can carry the cats to her?" Her nose wrinkled like someone was trying to feed her medicine.

"Your backpack's on wheels!" He lifted his arm out to her purple bag. "It won't be any heavier."

I wanted to sniff her bag, but Patch's tail was curling beneath him. I better not leave him.

"They're not mad at you," I said in his ear.

"Says you," said the girl back to the boy. Then she looked at me and Patch. "Why won't your sister come to school?"

"I don't want to talk about it."

The girl looked at JP again. "But you think she needs to see the cats."

"Yes! Like, infinity-needs-to!"

"Whoa. Okay. I'll take your books and stuff. But no trash."

"'Kay, great."

She unzipped her pack and took whatever he handed her, wedging things into her purple bag. More wrappers got stuffed in his pockets, even his shoes.

When JP's bag was emptied, he leaned it over to one side and lifted the top so I could see in. I sniffed the entrance. It was dark inside like a little den, and the walls were soft. Being carried in it wouldn't be fun, but it probably wouldn't be too bad. If he lived close by, the trip wouldn't take too long. And at the end of the journey, Patch would be where he needed to go, I was sure of it.

A piece of yellow cheese was lowered in front of my face. I sniffed it. Cheese wasn't my scene, but when JP set it inside the bag, I appreciated the thought. A little bribe never hurt a cat.

I took a step inside the bag. Patch mewed in alarm.

"You want to go in there?"

"Not really," I said. "But if it gets us to Nikki..."

Patch wailed. "If?"

"Aww!" said the girl.

"There's nothing to be afraid of." I studied JP's face again. It was drawn with worry and hope. He reminded me of a starving kitten I'd seen at the shelter once, who looked at things offered to her the same way, as if her entire world depended on the thing in front of her being food.

I stepped all the way inside the bag and kneaded the cloth floor with my claws. "He'll take care of us," I said.

Patch mrred, almost an anxious growl.

"JP, you can't separate him from his son!" said Marta.

"I won't."

Carefully, he took the edges of his bag and rotated it so the opening was upright. He went slow, so I never lost my footing. I sat in the bag, looking up at the sky through the open zipper before popping my head up to watch Patch.

"C'mere, kitty kitty," said JP. He reached under Patch's arms and began to lift him. Patch's ears flattened.

"Gingerrrr...."

"It's all right, stay calm, he's putting you in here with me..."

Patch moaned, but I thought he had it—until JP lowered him towards me.

The kit screamed. "NO, DON'T SHOVE ME IN THERE! I WON'T GO!" He twisted and in a whiskerflick erupted into a storm of claws.

"OW!" yelled JP. Red lines appeared across his hand.

Patch dropped to the ground and shot up the tree. I hopped out of the bag. The smell of fear-pee stank.

This was a mistake.

"Are you all right?" asked Marta.

"He got me good. Ow-ow-ow!" JP held his hand.

"I have hand sanitizer." She reached into the front of her purple bag.

I looked at the wound and flinched. Humans didn't tolerate cats scratching their children. Even if the boy wanted us for Nikki, his mother wouldn't after seeing that gash.

This was a BIG mistake.

I slunk to the tree while Marta poured nasty-smelling goo on JP's hand. He hissed in pain.

"I don't think you should try that again, JP. The little one peed on everything."

"How else am I supposed to sneak them home to her? Tomorrow's the last day before winter break and there's no way Mom's going to let me come back here alone. She just barely lets me walk home with you!"

"But you can't put them in a pack!"

"I can't buy a cage! I haven't had an allowance since we moved."

"Maybe...maybe..." She shook her head.

Thunder rumbled above our heads.

"My sister *needs* those cats."

He blinked hard and swiped his nose with his sleeve. Our eyes met again.

His sister. Nikki. That's who Patch is meant to be with.

I slow blinked at him. *I'm sorry. Don't give up.*

Rain began pattering down.

"I'll be back tomorrow," said JP, like he knew I understood what he was saying.

But Patch won't be ready by then, whispered my fear.

I climbed back up the tree.

* * *

Patch was all abristle when I arrived.

"See! He tried to stuff me in something. He's just like other humans. Cruel!"

Raindrops tapped against the leaves. I replayed what JP had done to Patch in my head. The pickup had been a little awkward —more like how Gina hauled me around when she was unsteady on baby feet—but Damien had taught her later how to support my feet so I felt better getting carried. Children could be taught. But JP hadn't yanked on him. And he did NOT stuff Patch anywhere.

"You panicked when he lowered you."

"It was so dark and small." His voice dropped. "I knew you were in there, but..." He went quiet. "It just...*reminded* me, you know?" He smushed his face into my chest, and I forgot to be mad at him. I purred until the softness came back into his shoulders and spine. Wasn't right for a kitten to have such fear, such bad memories. I'd never felt anything that bad, except maybe when it came to visiting the vet. Even just seeing the cage left out made me edgy and cranky, and of course I didn't like going in it, but I wasn't *scared* of it.

"He's coming back tomorrow," I said. "It'll be the last time you get to decide whether or not you go with him." I beat my tail once on the tree crook. "If you don't go with him, I don't know what happens to me."

"To you?"

"Yeah. My mission is to get you to your human, Nikki. If you refuse...I don't know. Maybe I get sent back. I don't want that. I think you're a good kit, Patch; I hate to think of you scrounging around these trees in the winter without anyone to look out for you."

The thunder rolled above our heads. Raindrops began pattering down.

"You mean...if I don't go, I'll be alone?"

"I'm not sure. I have 'til the Christmas snowfall to get you to your human. Maybe that's when I'll get taken back."

"You keep saying 'your human' 'your human'—how can a human belong to me? They're like, ten times bigger than me!"

I chuckled. "Oh, you'd be surprised. You can get them so trained, they wouldn't dare—" I stopped myself, watching his eyes light up with intrigue. "Well, it's really better for you to see it in action."

He grumbled, wiggled away.

"And I won't get to see any of it unless I go with that boy, huh?"

I smiled at him. He sighed, whisking his tail. He didn't say anything until the tree lights flickered on. He finally looked up from his paws.

"I'll think about it," he said.

The rain kept falling.

CHAPTER FOURTEEN

The next morning was just as pale and a little chillier than the one before, but it was dry. This time when the children began filing under our tree, Patch crept to the lower branches to observe. I sat hidden in the crook of the tree. Only Patch could make this choice. I couldn't be brave for him.

I started to doze. Then—was that strawberry milkshake I smelled?

"Hi, kitties!"

My ears twitched. It was Marta!

"See you after school! We love you!"

"Marta!" said the boy. I grinned without opening my eyes. Marie used that voice on Damien on occasion—usually after he or Gina made a joke about my litter box. "We don't want anyone to know!"

"That we love them?"

"That they're up there!"

Scuffle scuffle.

The kit touched his nose to mine. I opened my eyes.

"How can they love me if they don't know me?" he demanded. "I scratched him!"

I yawned. "Children forgive."

He sat with that a while. Then he asked: "*If* I wanted to go with them, what..." He washed his face furiously with a white paw. "What...will make it easier?"

I studied the branches above me, thinking.

"First, you have to remember that they're not cats. They don't think our same way about things. And every human is different. But at the very least, you can't bite or scratch them."

"But what if—"

I stopped him with a paw on his chest. "You can't. When they take you home Indoors, you'll be family. So you can't hurt them or your friends. Including dog friends."

"WHAAT?!"

I nodded. His eyes bugged out.

"Now, if a stranger comes into your house at night, scratch him up good!"

Patch brightened. "Yeah?"

"But everyone else you just keep an eye on."

"Hmm."

"I know. But your humans will watch out for you. Especially you, since you're small and cute. You'll want to purr a lot and let them pet you." I rolled over. "Maybe even rub your tummy!"

His ears flashed back. "In their dreams!"

"You don't have to do everything all at once. But if you want them to be YOUR humans, you'll have to let them know that you like them, even if you're not sure about trusting them."

"Hmm..." He frowned again. "I don't know."

CRACK went the sky over our heads. Patch dove under me, trembling. But no rain came.

"If I go to live with humans, will THAT stop happening?" he asked, head whipping about to monitor the whole sky.

"Nope," I said. "But you'll have a big warm bed to hide under."

The wind blew through our fur. Patch shivered.

"OK. I'll go down."

* * *

The wind let up later, helping us hear the *BRIIIING*! of the school bell. And though the sky was still gray as the children walked beneath our tree, the sky seemed to be brighter. At last, the main stampede was over, and a familiar voice called up the tree.

"Hi, kitties!"

Patch looked at me.

"You ready?" I asked.

"I don't want to go in the bag."

"Then we won't," I said. "Just follow my lead."

He nodded. "Right."

And then he scrambled down the tree ahead of me!

Maybe this will work!

I followed him.

JP—this time in a brown cap—sat at the bottom of the tree with his pack, while Marta stood, pulling her puffy jacket tight around her. She didn't have her wheelie bag with her.

"They're not gonna go in your pack, JP."

"I know, I ain't trying that!" JP pulled his lunch bag out of his pack. I sat back as Patch marched right over. JP took out a little plastic bowl and—memories flooded back—a turquoise can of cat food. White Persian on the label. Salmon smell wafted out of the can as he cracked it open. He barely had time to dump it in the bowl before Patch flung his face in to feast.

"Whoa! Slow down there, buddy!" said the boy. He rubbed Patch's back. Then, reaching into his pack he brought out...

Two leashes.

I winced. I'd heard of a few cats in Heaven who swore by those—said it'd let them guide their humans safely through their Outdoor adventures—but Gina had tried one on me once and it was DEFINITELY not my scene.

While Patch scarfed and gobbled, JP sneaked behind him and tried circling the collar loop around his neck.

But patch noticed.

"HEY!" he shouted. He turned on JP, hissing.

"Don't bite him!" I said, leaping over.

The boy threw up his hands, leash dangling. He backed up so fast he fell onto his bottom.

"What the heck was that?!" said Patch.

"A leash."

"What he was trying to do with it?"

"I think he wanted to walk you home."

"Like a DOG? A DOG SLAVE?"

"Well..." *Yeah, kinda.*

"No way! No how! Not on my last life!" Patch hopped up and down, spitting in fury.

Marta pulled the boy up. "JP, I'm sorry."

He swiped his arm across his eyes, but he couldn't hide his nose, red with crying. Without another look at us, he threw his backpack over his shoulder, leaving the bowl and leashes on the ground. The unzipped flap of his pack bobbed as he hurried away.

"Your sister wouldn't want a dangerous cat," my ears caught Marta saying as she ran after him.

"He's not dangerous!" said the boy.

I looked at Patch. His claws were back in. He stared at the retreating humans with enormous blue eyes. Disbelieving eyes.

"They're really leaving..." said Patch.

"They don't know how to bring you home," I said. *You won't let them,* I almost added.

I moaned, hanging my head. *He's just too scared, Lord.* What would happen to me? What would happen to him?

The kit glanced at the sky. Then—

Pa-pitta, pa-pitta!

"Wait! Don't leave without us!" cried Patch. I looked up. He was galloping after the children! I ran to his side. JP hadn't turned his head, but Marta looked back. When she saw us coming, her face lit up. "JP! He's following you!"

"Marta..."

"No, look!"

JP's head started to turn, but he shook himself and stared forward before he caught sight of me and Patch.

"Nuh-uh," he said.

"JP, I'm not kidding!"

Patch huffed and puffed, springing ahead of me until he was two cats' lengths behind them. He kept that length between them until they stopped at a tar road with white stripes banded across, like a bridge to the other safe path. When they stopped, Patch stopped. I trotted up next to him and sat while Marta watched.

"They're RIGHT. THERE."

JP pretended to look both ways for cars.

Marta grabbed his shoulders and spun him around. "Look, doggone it!"

JP was suddenly very interested in the cloudy sky.

"Hey!" said Patch. "Don't ignore us!"

JP jolted at the sound of Patch's mew. Finally, the boy looked down.

"They're following us?"

Marta rolled her eyes.

JP glanced across the tar road. Then he knelt down again, hand out to Patch. "C'mere!" He took a step forward. Patch took a step back.

JP stepped back towards the striped road. Patch stepped forward again.

JP stepped on one of the stripes. Patch and I stepped forward together. JP sighed.

"All right," he said. "Have it your way."

He crossed the road and we followed a few paces behind.

"You gotta keep your ears open when you cross the road," I told the kit. "Just as much as your eyes. Sometimes it's easier to hear fast cars coming than to see them. Look both ways, too."

JP kept turning his head to watch us, bumping into Marta.

"Why do I have to know this stuff if I'm going to be an Indoor cat?"

"Because we're not where we need to be yet."

We reached the safe path on the other side. I let Patch set the distance between us and the children the entire walk. We followed them around curving paths and across driveways and even crossed two more striped tar roads. When they stopped in front of a house with a light-up reindeer in the yard, we stopped, too. I gave Patch an approving lick.

"Do you..." started JP. "You'll have to keep them at your house."

I trilled in shock. We weren't taking Patch to Nikki?

"What?" said Marta. "you didn't say—"

"We live in Mom's cousin's RV now. Like, just until Mom gets a job and we move out. But anyway, no pets allowed 'til then. I'll buy the food!" He dug into his back pocket and pulled out a pawful of little cans. "Here. I'll get you more tomorrow. You just have to keep them."

"I think I could hide one cat maybe, but two? And what about Baba? She barks at any cat she sees, how'm I supposed to hide *that* from Mom?"

Marta had a dog? That milkshake lotion must be masking its scent.

"I saw online how to make a shelter from a plastic tub. Maybe..."

"Omigosh, JP, you are so...so...!"

"What about your shed? It's for a good cause—it's Christmas!"

She stuck a finger in his face. If she were a cat, I bet she would have had the claw out.

"You owe me."

He held out his palms, pushing the air away from him. "I know, I know! And I'll buy you a box of Snowballs."

"And kitty litter."

"Fine!"

"And tell me more about your sister."

JP paused. "I won't have to tell you about her. I'll bring her over to meet the cats."

Then, so softly I had to prick my ears, "If I can get her to come."

"What'd you say?" said Marta.

"Nothing. Never mind. You'll meet my sister. And you'll like her. I promise."

Marta gave him a final, wary look before saying a slow, "Okaaay..." and stuffing the cans into her jacket and pants pockets. Patch watched the movement of the cans, whiskers flexing.

When she had our food, Marta patted her leg and said in her kitty croon, "C'mon, kitties!"

I took a few steps toward her, but stopped. Patch wasn't following, but watching JP, who hadn't moved. I swirled around.

"Patch, over here," I said.

The kit kept his eyes on the boy. "I thought you said I was supposed to go to his sister."

JP took a step away and Patch took one to match it, towards JP, away from Marta.

"We're taking a detour," I said.

Patch's lip pooched out. "For an angel, you sure don't know much!"

You're telling me!

"It'll be okay. Marta's good people." I beckoned with my tail. He still didn't move. "Do I have to carry you like a milk-kneader?"

At last, Patch came over. Marta awwed at him through her mitten, then went up the driveway. Turning back to make sure we were following, she unlocked the gate leading to her backyard. I nudged Patch ahead, then looked over my shoulder at JP. He was walking away down the safe path. But before he went down the hill and out of sight, he looked back and our eyes met for a flash. He turned away quickly and hurried off.

"Kitty-kitty!" Marta called from the backyard. I waited one more second, hoping for a glimpse of JP's green hat—a glimpse I thought might bring understanding—or at least a hint that I was doing the right thing, that me and Patch really were at the right place. But JP was gone.

I turned around and followed Marta.

CHAPTER FIFTEEN

Instead of a hard gray floor, the shed was lined with dull tongue-colored carpet that puffed dust into your face when you walked on it. It left a sight feel of grit under my claws. The walls couldn't be seen because big plastic boxes had been stuffed in instead, on the floors and up on shelves, all except for the back corner, which was bare except for the carpet. I sniffed the perimeter of this bare space alongside Patch. *Cinnamon potpourri.* Just like Marie's boxes of Christmas. They'd been full of plastic pine scarves and blinky lights.

Above the bare corner, a little window illuminated the dusty carpet with a square of light from outside. I spotted the edges of blinky lights at the window corners, but they weren't on yet. It wasn't exactly cozy in here, but the walls, carpet and plastic bins kept the wind from whistling through our pelts.

Patch sneezed. A biff of dust shot into the air.

"Sorry, kitty, I don't think I can get a vacuum back here without Mom seeing," said Marta. She wedged a tub labeled EASTER in front of the bare corner, blocking it from view, but still allowing a gap so we could come and go.

She let go of it and stood back, huffing and puffing. "Guess you guys can use Baba's old drinking bowl...and I think she's got an extra food dish, too..."

Patch worked at tucking his paws under him, loafing in the center of the cleared space. Marta smiled at him before she bent and petted my head. Ahh.

"Be right back," she said.

The shed door closed behind her with a *creeeak*, rattling in the gust of wind.

"How you doing, kit?"

"Sooooft," he said.

Within seconds, he was snoring, his head bowed towards the carpet. I shook off the dust from my back paws and circled our mini territory again.

Kit can't live like this. It's not even a whole room to himself. How long will he have to be here? My tail curled and uncurled. Christmas would be here in just a few nights. He might be able to meet his human by then, but that wouldn't be the same as becoming a part of her family.

Creeeak.

I jumped. Patch startled awake, but didn't unloaf. The wind took a breath and in the silence I thought I heard a dog baying.

"Hi, kitties," said Marta. Arms full, she used her foot to scooch the Easter box aside. In the back corner she set a shallow cardboard box of shredded paper, like from Damien's office. She touched Patch's nose, earning her a dirty look, but thankfully no scratches.

"You potty here," she said, tapping her finger in the shredded paper box. "JP's gotta get you real litter but I hope this'll work for the night." I sniffed the pictures of tomatoes on the side of the makeshift litterbox while she set a huge bowl of water down. She tapped a fresh can of food into a giant dish next to it and Patch slunk directly to it. If it had been a dog's dish, I couldn't smell the scent on it; it must have been a while before it was last used.

"Hey, leave some for him. C'mon!" She gently picked him up. Patch squealed in protest.

"Hush, hush!" she said to him. "Time to eat," she said to me.

It smelled good, but I really wasn't hungry. I sniffed it to be polite, then climbed into her lap, purring. She released Patch to eat while she cuddled me, cooing the whole time. It relaxed me so that I almost missed what she said before she left us.

"Baba potties in the backyard later. She might bark, but don't be scared, she can't get in. You boys just stay quiet."

She pulled the Easter box back into place, then set some roly-poly looking black trash bags on top of it, building a taller wall around our space. A human would have to come back here and peek past the Easter box to see us.

"I'll see you in the morning after Mom goes to work. Love you, kitties."

I gave her a slow blink. Patch gave a last lick of his food and then went to the center of the carpet to loaf.

Hm. Maybe he hadn't listened to those tips I gave him as well as I thought he had.

The sky darkened. The blinky lights outside came on, pouring cozy orange, pink, and green light into our nest in the shed. Patch used the strange litterbox without a problem. After he settled back in, I joined him, loafing close so our bodies pressed together, sharing warmth.

I looked down at the blaze on my chest. The miracle stripe had disappeared. *Must have happened when I rescued him from the car.*

Which meant I had one more miracle left. But I couldn't figure out how to use it.

The wind had faded. Now the constant barking of a dog floated in the air, continuing even after a human shushed it. I trained my half-lidded gaze on the food and water dish. Baba's things.

Patch grumbled in his sleep, kneading my side.

Well, Lord, we're not where we're supposed to be, but I suppose we're closer than we were yesterday.

I laid my head on my paws and fell asleep.

* * *

My ears perked at Marta and JP's muffled whispers outside the shed.

Click click. Creeeak.

I peeled open an eye. Whoa. Still dark out. But my angel clock inside me told me it was one day closer to Christmas. I stretched.

"Whuz?" said Patch, next to me. He swiped his face with his paw.

Human footsteps approached us on the carpet. JP removed the trash bags and Marta slid the Easter box over. They worked together to empty the paper litter tray, and JP poured fresh sand in from a green bag.

"All right!" said Patch, trotting over to see.

"Is your sister coming today?"

"No," said JP, petting Patch's rump. The kit glanced back at him, but after a look from me, ignored the boy, sniffing the clean litter.

"Good," said Marta, scooping me into her lap.

"What?!" said JP.

"You don't have to look like that."

"I'm not looking like anything!"

"Yes you are. Anyway, I want to meet your sister, duh, but I think first I better introduce Baba O'Reilly to the cats. She barked her head off all last night at them. I had to lie and tell my parents it was because of the wind."

"She doesn't bark at the wind?"

"Not really, but this isn't the first time she's gone crazy for no reason. We think she's part bloodhound, smelling stuff we can't." She touched her face. "She's old but she's still got a nose."

"You think it's safe? For them to meet, I mean?"

"I'll keep her on her leash, but I want you to help with the cats. Make sure they don't run out the door."

"Right now?" asked JP.

"No—later. When she gets back from the groomer's. Mom'll drop her off here before she goes to work. If you're quiet you can just stay in the shed until she leaves again. You could play with the kitties so they're more used to you."

That sounds like a great idea.

I hopped out of Marta's lap and put a paw on JP's leg. The silly boy had worn shorts today, but his leg was warmer than I thought it'd be.

"You want me to stay and play, boy?" He scratched behind my ears. I purred and smiled up at him.

"OK," he said to Marta. "I'll stay."

"Great. Mom'll be back in ten. Then I'll bring Baba out to you."

Marta crawled out our secret corner, replaced the Easter box, then the garbage sacks.

Creeeak, went the shed door, and we were left with JP in the shed.

He pulled a crinkly mouse out of his pocket. Patch froze, the leg he'd been grooming still in the air.

"Ha! See the mousie?" JP made it crinkle again.

Patch stalked over.

"It's fuzzy like a mouse," he said after batting it, "but it's not a mouse."

"It's a toy," I said. I picked it up by its tail and Patch came over to sniff it again.

"Do you eat it?"

"I wouldn't. No meat in it. Just white fuzz that sticks to your tongue."

I dropped it. Patch batted at it once, twice, double-cleaning-paw-THWAP! Then he grabbed it up, rolled onto his belly and went to town on it using his back paws. JP was grinning.

"Aw, man, this is great!" said Patch. "We got all the food, a place to stay out of the cold, and a soft floor."

JP tried to pet Patch while the kit walked by, but the little fink slunk his spine under so when JP's hand came down, he didn't feel any of Patch's soft fur. Patch wedged himself between a couple of tubs, where JP couldn't reach him, toy mouse still in his mouth.

"Patch!"

"Whumf?"

"You're supposed to let humans pet you."

He let the mouse toy drop onto the carpet. "Like, more than once?"

"Absolutely! You want your humans to belong to you, right?"

Patch screwed up his face, appraising JP. "I...guess."

"Then you have to get used to them petting you. Here, watch." I walked between Patch and JP, brushing the boy's leg with my tail. Then I flopped over on my side. The boy took the bait and began rubbing my tummy. A little hard, so I stuck a soft foot up to push his hand away. He began petting my side instead. Patch came out of his hidey spot to watch.

"If you really don't like how someone's petting you—if they don't stop when you give 'em a signal—you can give 'em a little smack," I said. "Some cats will tell you to bite them. But it's easier to just roll over or turn around. See?"

JP had started on my tummy again, so I rolled back upwards to demonstrate. Predictably, his hand moved to my back. Then I stood up and faced the boy. He began petting between my ears. Ahh.

"See? Offer different parts, they get the idea."

"Hmm," said Patch.

"It might take you a while to get used to it. So when you're done, you just walk away." I stood up and padded out of reach of the boy. As predicted, JP's hand went back to his knee. "The more you trust a human, the longer you'll feel comfortable letting them pet you. It's worth the time you put in."

JP reached for the mouse again. Patch looked like he was going to say something, but then the shed door rattled.

BARK! BARK!

Patch fled to his hidey spot. I jumped to the passageway by the Easter box to see, claws digging into the dusty carpet.

"Who's in there?" said a voice. "I can smell you. I ain't dead yet!"

"Baba, hush!" said Marta on the other side of the door.

"You better not be messing with my pack's stuff!"

Creeeak!

A huge dog charged in.

CHAPTER SIXTEEN

The brown dog's ears flapped as she zoomed straight for me. She jammed her snout in the gap, sniffing like a vacuum cleaner.

"Um...hi," I said, once I realized no teeth were coming, just sniffing. "My name's Gingersnap Cat. What's yours?"

"Hold on...just a sec..." White fur sprinkled her jowls, which wobbled as she sniffed. Marta hauled on the leash, but the dog wasn't bothered.

Finally, the sniffing stopped. "Just where are you from, anyhow?" she demanded.

"I'm an angel. From Heaven," I said.

The dog's hindquarters thunked to the floor. "Well, I'll be a flea's buggy-ride. It was driving me crazy, that smell was—well, not the smell exactly, but the not figurin' it out. THAT was more annoying than pepper in your jowls. Now, what was it you were saying?" Her tail swung like a branch in a lazy wind.

"I'm Gingersnap, ma'am. That young cat over there is Patch."

"He ain't no angel!"

I grinned. "That's right. He's a regular cat. But he's also special. The Lord wants him—I think—to go live with the boy's sister." I flicked my tail towards JP. "But Patch has never lived Indoors before and, uh, is working on his human-handling technique."

"And you've been sent to help him! Well, good for you."

My fur puffed as the huge brown dog leaned over, but all she did was give me a lick—a really gooshy lick, but still, a kindly one.

"I'm Baba O'Reilly, but y'all just call me MeMe. Sonny! C'mon out! Let MeMe have a sniff atcha. Eyes aren't what they used to be," she said to me.

I turned to Patch's shadowy corner and nodded.

"Wow. They're getting along!" said Marta as the kit crept out.

"Ohh, ain't he darling," said Baba the dog. "Like a little sugar cube!" Her tail started wagging again.

Patch raised his nose to her. His hackles were raised, but they sniffed nose to nose without him clawing her. Baba lay down, her long front legs extending into our area. The fur was worn off her elbows from lying on human floors for so many years. The same had happened to me years before I got sick.

She watched as Marta went to pet Patch. Again, the kit maneuvered his back quarters so the girl couldn't touch him. Baba turned to me, silent, but question clear in her eyes.

I sighed. "I know. He could be better with them."

Her floppy ears jumped. "Could be better? I'll say! Young cat. Young cat. Tell me about yourself."

Patch scampered over. I didn't think he could talk if he wanted to, but he surprised me and answered: "Um...My name's—"

"Closer, son! I can't hear ya!"

He minced a little bit closer, and when he spoke, he spoke louder than usual. "My name's Patch. My mom got taken away by humans—"

"Oooh," crooned the dog.

"—but Gingersnap says I'm supposed to live with humans now. He *thinks*."

"You ain't lived with humans yet, sonny?"

Patch shook his head.

"How do you like 'em so far? ...Go on!" she added, lowering her head to the floor when he didn't answer right away. I waited a few seconds, but when he still didn't reply, I prodded him with my paw. (Marta giggled again.)

"Uh...They're...Idunno. They're big! And they pet rough."

"The children usually do. But they don't stay small forever." Baba sighed, looking back at Marta. "No, sir, they sure don't."

Marta scratched behind where the big dog's floppy ears attached. "It's that better, Baba? See, they're just kitties. Not raccoons or anything."

"Well...I guess if they don't pet rough forever, I could like them. This Indoors stuff isn't too bad now."

Deep lines covered the dog's brow. "How do you figure?"

"Well, there's"—he kneaded the carpet—"soft stuff. And food! It's not too bad. I could get used to Indoors. I just don't know if I like having all the people around, that's all."

Baba wuffed, flews flapping. "You think this is living Indoors?" She turned to me. "You been telling him THIS is Indoors?"

"Well, it's, um, more than Indoors than—"

She turned back to Patch, the quickness of the motion making her ears slap against her teeth. "This ain't living Indoors!" she said to him. "And this ain't living with humans!"

Patch glanced at me, alarmed. "It's not?"

"No! For Heaven's sake—No offense—"

"None ta—"

"But if you think living in a junk shed is Indoors, you're crazy. Where's your bed? Your couch? Your TV set? Where's the people you cuddle? Or their bed to cuddle on? And TOYS!"

Patch stared up at her, jaw hanging loose. Marta and JP watched the rumbling, barking, wao-waoing dog.

"You haven't caught the scent of it, not the *real* notion of living Indoors. Young cat, if you are willing to let humanfolk into your heart, you will have a life bigger and better'n you have room in your head to dream!

"I know you're scared 'cuz you been on the alley and everything. I was born in a shelter, but raised in a human pack my whole life. So I can't say I know I understand you all the way. But if you keep your heart closed like an alley cat, the best you'll ever get is a shed. Where ferals live. But Heaven saw fit to send you an angel. I reckon that means you're meant for bigger and better than a shed. You could have a pack—I mean, a real family! Heaven sent you help, so live up to it. Let my girl and her friend handle you a little. They're good pups. You don't have to turn into a dog! You're a cat and you're different and that's OK. But think about your heart being open like a door; not solid like a wall. Got it?"

Patch blinked his wide blue eyes.

"Yes, ma'am."

"Good. Now come over here and let MeMe give you a kiss."

The kitten went with his head bowed. He sat in front of the wise hound and received his slurpy lick on top of his head. It rolled him over and she nuzzled his fluffy tummy with her large dark nose. She stood to leave. "Now if you'll excuse me, my stories are on."

Without another word, she turned and left for the shed door, Marta trailing on the leash.

JP leaned back against the plastic tubs, watching Baba and Marta leave the shed.

"What the heck was that about?" the boy said to himself.

* * *

From then on, Patch didn't twist his spine out of alignment when JP petted him. He even let Marta put him in her lap, though he crawled out before he warmed her lap any. I hurried over to take his place.

Mmm...Marta's not half bad at this. I found myself dozing as she massaged my forehead and mouth whiskers.

I felt little blue eyes on me and peeked open an eye. Patch studied us from a crouch a tail-length away. He didn't move when JP began scratching his rump again, but he didn't purr, or acknowledge the boy. Still, it was progress from this morning.

"Does it really feel that good?" he asked me.

"Mmm...hm!"

"And you're not 'fraid she's gonna hurt you?"

"Mmm...nope!" I said through my purr.

"But how do you know?"

I thought that one over a while. Marta rubbing my whiskers had nothing to do with the delay. "I have good instincts. And I trust people." I stretched a paw in the air and my claws extended out. But Marta didn't react. Some of Gina's friends used to, thinking claws out always meant trouble. "You don't have to trust all people, Patch. But us alley cats have good instincts. What are yours telling you?"

He didn't answer. But when JP sat next to him, he didn't move away.

CHAPTER SEVENTEEN

Breakfast was late the next day. At first, Patch hadn't worried. He just turned over to snooze longer. But as the day grew brighter, he began scratching at the plastic tub walls. *Cree, cree!* went his claws against the plastic. I tried my best to ignore it, but the sound was worse than litter between your toes.

"Are you trying to dig us out?" I asked.

"What if they don't come back? We'll be trapped here!"

"They'll come back, Patch. When humans leave the house for a while like this they're usually at work or school or the movies. It's the time for napping, not destroying their stuff like a puppy." Not that the thick plastic was at all bothered by his needley claws.

"We could starve to death!"

"We won't starve, Patch. They're coming back—have faith in them. You'd almost think you liked having humans around."

I brushed my tail against his face. He tried to bite it but I pulled it away easily.

"I like 'em when they bring food, but I NEED them when they're the only ones who can let us back Outdoors!"

My ear flicked. "You want to live Outdoors again? Hunting your own food and being cold?"

"I don't...maybe a little...but the dog said I was special, to have an angel!"

He began attacking his own tail.

Poor kit. If he'd just relax and believe us, he'd be fine.

I hopped up and grabbed his toy mousie. "Why don't you take your mind off things for a while?" I dropped it and batted it into his whirlwind tail fight. He looked up at me, clearly insulted.

"I don't know why you're not taking this seri—"

The latch rattled. I sniffed. Basketball rubber, strawberry milkshake...and hesitation, sadness, doubt. Who had the children brought with them?

Creeeak.

"They're in here," said JP. "You have to move slow and be quiet. The little one is shy."

I rushed over to Patch and began licking him down.

"He only really let me pet him yesterday," JP went on. "And that was only a little...you'll have to go slow."

"John Paul...!" said a new voice. I stopped grooming Patch. Was that JP's name, too?

"John Paul Daly, if you're tricking me, you'd better watch it! I'll go straight to Mom. And you know it!"

My ears followed the song of this new voice. It was different than any other human's voice I'd heard. Not just slower, but with a kind of a drawl that made the sentences weavy.

"No tricks, Nikki. I promise."

The Easter bin got pushed aside. Nikki was taller—yes, and older!—than both JP and Marta. Her blonde hair was pulled into a ponytail. She looked around, then her gaze dropped to the floor. When she saw me and Patch, a grin spread across her face, on one side more than the other in a way that I'd never seen before. Her eyes didn't quite focus, either. She looked a little peculiar, to be honest. But she smelled safe, and the first thing she did was sit down slowly.

"Hi, babies!" She had turned her voice into a whisper, one my ears liked. I gave her a slow blink and purred. She leaned forward just a little, so her hands were flat on the floor in front of her.

Next to me, Patch rose up, his hind feet flat on the ground. Nikki's hand flew to her mouth, trying to stifle a delighted squeal.

"Go on," I said to him. After a moment, he went back on all fours and padded to her.

"What's his name?" she asked, petting him with one finger. She touched him as though he were a cloud, the softest handling of all the children so far.

JP and Marta looked at each other.

113

"We haven't given either of them names," said Marta at the same time JP said, "I wanted you to name them."

Nikki gasped. After a pause that was longer than I was used to, she asked, "I get to name them?"

"Yeah," said JP.

"JP..." warned Marta, but he waved her off. This whole time his eyes were locked to his sister's face, and he was smiling. There was no pain in his hope now.

Nikki ran her finger over Patch's back. She traced the splotch on his back. "He's got a little...a little...rrrgh...thing that horses wear. What's the word?!" She hissed the question to herself, under her breath, but it was still loud. A dull, frustrated look settled heavily on Nikki's face.

"A saddle?" said Marta.

The heavy look disappeared. "Yeah! He has a saddle...and a hat." Nikki scritched the gray marking between his ears. "He's a...a cowboy! That's the word. Hi, Cowboy," she said to the kit. He looked up at her, straight into her eyes. For three heartbeats, neither of them moved.

I think that was the moment when he got it.

He made no move to leave when she cupped him in her hands and lifted him against her heart to cuddle. Marta gave the softest gasp. But Patch—Cowboy, now—buzzed a happy purr as Nikki ran her hand over his back.

"Nikki. What do you want to name him?" JP pointed to me.

Nikki looked me over with narrow eyes. They darted up, held there. Then she looked at Patch again. "Bronco," she said with a grin.

JP laughed.

Nikki stuck her chest out. "What? What? You got a problem with that, little bro?"

"No. It's just...you barely looked at him!"

"Pff." She held three fingers up, like Gina used to do to show counting. "Whatever!"

"Yeah, you're right. What's a cowboy without his horse?"

A bronco is a horse? Damien left TV on for me (well, he did if Marie didn't catch him and turn it off before work), but I mostly used it to help me fall asleep. So my TV memories were fuzzy— but could you blame me? If I'd known I was coming back and able to understand humans better, I would have paid more attention and napped less!

Maybe.

I padded up to Nikki. Time to give her the sniff over.

The smell of sadness had faded since she saw the kit. Her shampoo smelled like oranges, and her clothes were a little worn. But her lap was warm and comfy. I sprawled across it, purring my approval.

Ka-chink! I looked over to find Marta holding her rectangle up at us.

"I thought that was supposed to be for emergencies," said JP.

Nikki gave a croak. But when I checked on her I realized it was a wonderful laugh. Patch was sniffing her neck, whiskers brushing against her. My Gina had been ticklish there, too.

Marta shoved her rectangle in JP's face. "But look how cute! If I didn't get a pic of that I would've died and that would've been an emergency."

"Yeah, JP," said Nikki. "She could have DIED."

I yawned. Typical girl exaggeration-for-effect. I'd seen it at all the sleepovers.

JP's eyes read the rectangle. "I guess if I ever needed proof that these cats are good for Nikki, this'd be it," he said.

"Hey, um...what's your name again?" said Nikki.

Marta smiled. "Marta."

"Yeah, Marta, can I see?"

She passed the rectangle to Nikki. What she missed was JP's stunned expression. From the way he was gawping at his sister, I got the feeling Nikki asking people for things didn't happen very often.

Nikki touched the rectangle with her finger. "Cowboy," she said softly. Then, turning the kit around, she showed him the rectangle. "Look, Cowboy. It's us! And Bronco. Heehee." She snuggled him again.

"Hey, Nikki?"

"What?"

"You wanna feed 'em?" JP popped the top off a can. Smelled like salmon from here. Near him was a plastic container.

"Yeah!" She set Patch down and listened intently as her brother gave her instructions. I crawled off Nikki's lap, over to Patch.

"How you doing, kit?"

"She's my human, isn't she?" said Patch.

Smiling, I nodded.

"It's weird...she wants me, just like the others, but..." his tail swished.

"She needs you, too," I finished for him.

His ears and tail perked. "That's it! And I know I can help her. I'll watch over her. Oh, and now she's feeding me?" He sprang for the food dish Nikki had prepared.

"This is great," he said between bites. "We can be a family, can't we, Gingersnap?"

I opened my mouth to reply, but then, the shed door went *creeeak!*

There in the doorway stood a dark-haired woman. Her arms went to her hips. "Marta Mariana Rivera, what is going on in here?"

CHAPTER EIGHTEEN

Patch dove under me. Marta turned red as an ant.

"Mom!" she said. "What are you doing home?"

"Today is our Christmas movie day. I got off work specially for it! But I see you forgot. Young man, who are you, and why are you here in our shed?"

"Um...my name's JP, Mrs. Rivera."

"Oh!" I was happy to see the woman's face softened. "From school?"

He nodded, nodded. She stepped forward and shook his hand. "It's good to finally meet you. Marta talks about you all the time."

Marta turned redder.

"A-and this is his sister, Nikki. They came over to see the cats."

"Yes! Marta, you know the pet rule—Baba's it until she passes."

"Oh, I know," said Marta. "But, see...these..." her pink-mittened hands flapped around as she flibbered and flabbered with her mouth.

"I asked Marta if we could keep the cats here—Just for a little while! My sister, um, she needs these cats, but our family's staying in a cousin's RV right now and we can't have any pets until we get a new apartment."

Mrs. Rivera's hand went to her lips. "I see." Patch's head peeped out.

"Knock knock," said a deep voice.

Patch's head retreated beneath me.

"What's the holdup, *mi amor*?" said the man to Marta's mother. "Did I miss a Christmas box, please-tell-me-I-didn't?" But his eyes were taking us in.

"No, Sam. Marta's friends have some new pets who've been staying in our shed."

"Oh!" said Marta's dad. "That explains Baba's barking a couple nights back. But she's hardly made a peep since then, except at the UPS man..."

"We introduced them," said Marta. "She likes the kitties."

Mr. Rivera smiled. "Well, I'll be. Guess you can teach an old dog new tricks."

"They just need a place to stay for the holidays," said JP.

"Until they get an apartment," said Marta.

"Oh? When are you moving in?" asked Mr. Rivera.

"Soon! Soon," said JP. But from the look the Riveras exchanged, they could smell the lie.

"Well, we're not ones to throw out strays on the holidays," said Mr. Rivera, "but Marta's grandma is taking us on a three-week cruise starting the day after Christmas."

"Oh, yeah!" said Marta.

"So you'll need to find them housing after the twenty-fifth. Think you can do that?"

"Oh, yes!" nodded JP, but I could smell the nerves in his sweat.

"That all right, Mama?" Mr. Rivera asked his mate.

"I guess so. I mean, I had no idea you even had them out here! And you're taking care of their poo-poos?"

"Yes, Mrs. Rivera," said JP.

"Yes, Mom," said Marta.

"Then I guess we can work with that. But honey, don't you want to go to the movies?"

"Well..." Marta's eyes flitted from me, to her friends, to her parents.

"Senior team meeting," said Mrs. Rivera suddenly. The door shut behind them.

"'Senior team meeting'?" said JP.

"Code for parent talk. Me and Baba are junior team members. What? Your family doesn—"

"No." JP stifled a smile with his hand, but it wasn't much use, the grin crawled out on either side of his fingers.

"NO-oh," echoed Nikki, rolling her eyes. She began patting the floor. "Cowboy. C'mere."

He scooted around beneath me, ready to go to her, but the door opened again and he froze beneath me.

"Marta, would your friends like to join us for our Christmas movie?"

Marta grinned with all her teeth. "They can come?"

"If they want. And if they get permission from their parents."

"Just Mom," muttered JP.

"Guys? Do you?" said Marta.

"A movie?" Nikki stared at Marta with something like awe. "You want me to go to a movie? With you?"

"Yeah? Why not?"

"I...I talk funny."

"Pssh!" Marta waved her away.

"I'll be right with you, Nikki," said JP. "We can check in on the cats after."

I yawned to show how relaxed Patch and I were. *We got this, guys. Go have fun.*

"Nnn...okay!"

"Can I use your phone, Mrs. Rivera?"

* * *

"Their mother must have said yes," I told Patch later after my bath.

"Wow, movies take a long time," said Patch.

121

"Yes. I like it better when they come back from the library. They bring books back from there, which means they have to sit down. And if there's room for a book near their lap, there's room for a cat on it."

"Sounds nice."

"Their hands taste like butter after the movies sometimes, though. Pros and cons." I stretched.

"If things are this nice with my Nikki now...what will they be like when I'm living with them?"

"Beyond better. It's like what Baba said: you can't even dream of it now. But you're on the right track, kit."

The question was, how were they going to keep him? They would have to find a new place to live, and that was a big ways trickier for a human family than a cat. I could remember moving with Damien and Marie, before they had Gina. What a ball of chaos! My favorite things and spots all replaced with boxes I couldn't sit inside...and then a long car ride...

Creeeak.

The children bounded into the shed. Patch headed towards his hidey hole until he saw Nikki's outstretched palms. Then he toddled right up to her to be picked up.

"Fuzzy Christmas, Cowboy!" she said.

Someone scrubbed my shoulders. "Fuzzy Christmas, Bronco," said Marta.

"JP. JP. Tell them the good news. Tell the kitties," said Nikki.

"You try, Nikki. See what you can remember."

She stuck her tongue out. "Fffiiine." Nikki directed her words to Patch. "Tomorrow afternoon, Marta's dad is taking us to the CHRISTMAS FAIR. And we get to take you kitties! And...and...Baba...Baba something."

"What's Baba going to help the kitties do?" Marta asked.

"...Oh! That's it. Baba will help you wear leashes."

Auggh, no!

"'Cuz you need a leash, Cowboy!" She slowly wagged her finger in his face. He tried to sniff it. "No running away."

Ha. Maybe only Patch would have to wear one.

"We'll work on that in the morning," said Marta. "Before Baba's nap." Then she handed a funny bag to Nikki. It was stiff like an upright box, but it had handles like Gina's library book bag. And it was a strange color—pink, but clear, like it was made of gummi bear stuff.

"And if you get tired, you can sit in here."

Then, without any ceremony of coaxing, Nikki plopped Patch into the bag!

Even I tensed along with the other children as Patch looked out as us from the confines of the pink gummi bag. He'd scratched and spitted at the backpack bag, and I'd been in it waiting for him!

Patch pawed the pink-tinted walls, checked the view out each side, then curled up, awaiting Nikki's next move.

"Whoa!" said Marta. "I never dreamed a jelly bag could be a miracle!"

I checked my blaze on habit. But of course that miracle stripe was long gone, and I hadn't felt anything funny when Patch entered the jelly bag.

I went over and stood up, looking into the bag. "Kit, you okay?"

"Sure. It's not dark in here. I can see everything!"

Nikki's hands gently scooched me away. She picked up the bag with Patch still in the bottom of it. Slipping it on, she looked back over her shoulder in a fancy pose.

Ka-chink! went Marta's rectangle. "So chic!" she said.

"Oo-la-laa!" said Nikki.

"Vut a fancee kittay, Madame!" said Marta. Then both girls laughed. From inside the bag, Patch raised an eyebrow at me.

No clue. I shrugged back.

Then I motioned over my own shoulder, where JP watched his sister with a happy smile. *But does it matter when they're all so happy?*

That night the children tucked us in without moving the Easter box, promising to come back in the morning. They told us not to be afraid of the leashes.

Hm, I thought. *We'll see how that goes, Lord. But You kept the lions from eating Daniel, so I guess if anyone can get a couple of cats to take leashes, it'd be You.*

Still, I'd love to see how He was going to do it.

CHAPTER NINETEEN

"This isn't working," said Marta the next morning.

I lay perfectly still on the dusty carpet, stifling sneezes, hoping if I were still enough, this silly thing they'd wrapped around me would go away.

"Is it really that bad?" Patch asked, sniffing my nose.

"Of course it ain't! He's just an ol' cat, and ol' cats are harder to teach new tricks than us ol' dogs!" said Baba. Her tail thumped the carpet, sending out a wave of dust my nose couldn't ignore. I sneezed.

"Bless you, Bronco," said Marta. Nikki stuck a cat treat in front of my nose. That was her job—to give me a treat every time I moved in this contraption.

I closed my eyes, ignoring the treat. *Lord, I want to be a good example for Patch, but this feeling—it's not natural!* Although it was better than the walking collar Gina had put on me—once.

That had felt like it was going to strangle me any minute. This just felt weird.

"Ol' MeMe's been walking on leashes longer'n you been alive," the old hound told Patch. "You got to start young." She began pawing Marta. "Somebody get it off the ginger and put it on the li'l one. He'll pick it up in no time."

"All right, Grandma," said Marta, thumping the dog on her back. "We'll do it your way." Marta pushed the old dog away and undid the cloth jacket things around my neck and tummy. *Scrotch scrotch*, they went as they pulled apart. Once free, I leaped onto JP's shoulder and pitoned my claws into his sweater.

"You're wearing him to the fair!" said Nikki. She laughed like there was no better joke. Me, I liked it up here. And I certainly wasn't going to run away—I had a job to do!

"OK, Patch, your turn..." said Marta, approaching him with the red vest.

Patch froze. "Uhh, Gingersnap?"

"Marta, Marta," said Nikki. "Cowboy's my kitty. I'll dress him."

"You sure? He might scratch."

Nikki gave her such a glare! Marta handed the vest over. She offered her palm to Patch, who came right over. She offered him the vest to sniff.

"It didn't hurt, did it?" he asked.

"No."

"Heavens, pup—pardon me again, Sir Angel—leashes don't hurt 'less you're fooling about with 'em. Stay still and let her put it on you. And that ain't even a leash proper, I reckon that's like a Christmas sweater, and those are darnright pleasant to wear in this chilly weather."

Nikki had wrapped it around Patch. *Scrotch, scrotch*, went the fasteners as it closed around him. I leaned over to watch. Patch lay still for the moment.

"Looks like it fit him better than you, Tom Angel. Now go on and tell me that don't feel like a hug. You can't, can you? 'Cuz it done feel just like a hug, like my Christmas sweater."

"It's...different. But not bad."

"Can you stand up? Stand up for MeMe," said the dog.

"Stand up for Nikki," I said.

"*Mewf!*" The kit threw himself on all fours. Treats showered down at his feet.

"GOOD BOY!" crooned Nikki. "GOOD GOOD BOY!"

Patch snarfed the treats down. Breakfast—and I hadn't gotten any. Good thing I didn't *have* to eat anymore. But the treats sure smelled tasty.

"There you go. See how happy you made your pack! Go on, now walk a little!"

Patch moved his arms and legs like they were branches, claws hooking into the carpet. Nikki patted his rump while sticking her three-treat-deep palm in front of his nose.

"GOOD COWBOY!"

"You look like you caught my rheumatism," said Baba. "Relax a little. It's a nice warm hug. Nothing to fluff your fur over."

Slurp. "Okay," said Patch through his full mouth. He ventured towards me and JP, now jerking his paws up unnaturally high.

"Hey, buddy!" said JP in a decent croon. "Want your mousie?" He held it up by its tail.

Patch sat and batted at it. Marta leaned over to give him treats but Nikki said, "Nuh uh," and dangled a long string in front of Patch instead.

Patch's eyes went dark with excitement, and his head twitched. Nikki was a natural at playing String! She wobbled and jerked it so well even I had a tough time not going after it. Patch, being so young, dove and leaped for it like she had a tuna fillet tied to the end!

By the time Patch stalked off with the string in his mouth, he was moving as smoothly as any cat in their natural fur.

"You may not be an angel, MeMe," I said to the hound, "but you're definitely a miracle worker!"

"*Aww-ooa,*" she said. "'Tweren't nothing." But then she turned away to scratch her ear, hiding her face from me.

"Cowboy can go to the Christmas Fair!" said Nikki.

"I think he can," said JP.

"But what about Bronco? We don't want him running away, and he won't take a leash."

"A *walking jacket,* JP," said Marta. "It's right on the box."

He waved her off. "Whatever it is, he won't wear it. If there's... Idunno, reindeer—"

"Reindeer?!" Marta's eyebrows shot up high.

"Like a petting zoo, hello? Anyway, if he sees something and freaks out, what stops him from running away? He doesn't have a collar yet, we could lose him."

"He followed us here without a leash."

"I'm serious! Maybe it's safer if we leave him behind. Nikki can take Cowboy and you can take Baba. He can stay here."

I sighed. *This would be a lot easier if humans and animals could just talk to each other.*

I climbed off JP's shoulder and went to the funny pink jelly bag. Stepping my feet very high, I got in. It was a little small on me, so my head stuck out the top. I looked JP in the eye. "I'm going. Even if you have to carry me," I told him.

Nikki clutched her head and fell over laughing.

"JP! Bronco's gonna make you wear a PURSE!" she said. And that was all it took to start Marta and Baba howling with laughter.

* * *

The ride over to the fair wasn't half bad, but by the time we were unpacked from the car I was ready to stretch my legs. I clambered onto JP's shoulder, leaving him holding the empty jelly bag.

"You're going to have to hold it, JP," said Marta, getting Baba out of the car. "In case he gets tired of riding you."

JP sighed and slung the bag over his shoulder.

"Thanks," I said, purring and rubbing his cheek. That stole a smile from him.

"All right, kids, Pastor Wade and your mom said they were meeting us by the wooden elf in the front," said Mr. Rivera. "Let's go."

Marta led the way with her father, holding on to Baba's leash. The brown dog wore a green sweater with a pattern that reminded me a little of Christmas trees. Nikki, holding Patch in his jacket, followed them while JP and I brought up the rear. I sniffed the air as we walked. It was cool, but not snow-cold today. The sky was even blue. We walked on a road with car-box-lines on it, but I could smell plenty of grass—and humans—and cooking—up ahead. And if I stood up straight, I could see trees in the distance. Was this a park?

We stepped onto a safe white path, then stood around with some other humans in a line before Marta's father handed over the important-smelling green paper to a lady. Then the safe road turned into a big grassy field. The smells were mixed and more intense here. Paths led between strange human building-boxes with toys and smelly pinecones and foods and other things. Christmas trees filled with lights sometimes stood in place of the building. But instead of going down one of these paths between the goodie-boxes, we veered off next to a flat wooden sign. There stood a short man who had yellow hair as bright as a cloud, and a woman with a worn face who smelled like Nikki. When the man saw us he waved, and a smile spread across his face, bright as his hair. It made me purr to see it, but Nikki suddenly ducked behind me and JP.

Marta ran up to the yellow-haired man and hugged him. "Pastor Wade!"

"Heya, Marta! Hi, Sam."

"Merry Christmas, Pastor." Marta's father turned to the worn woman. "Hi, I'm Sam Rivera, Marta's dad." They shook hands. "You must be JP and Nikki's mom. My wife's here somewhere," he held out his arms, "managing the kettle corn booth, though I hope for heaven's sake she's not eating as much of it as she's passing out!"

"Thank you for inviting us," said JP and Nikki's mom. "You can call me Christine."

Pastor Wade came up to JP. Still smiling, he nodded at me. "Is this the surprise?"

"Wha?" said JP, smiling back.

"Your Mom told me you had a surprise for her. Is this cat it?"

JP pulled the brim of his neon yellow hat down over his face.

"Yeah, I thought so," said the pastor with a wink. Then he leaned around to see Nikki. As bad as JP was, she was holed up in her jacket like a frightened mouse.

The pastor looked at her a second, then squatted down at Cowboy's level. "And who are you, little guy?"

Nikki's eyes plead with JP's, but her brother crossed his arms. She said something.

"Chowder?" asked the pastor.

"NO! Cowboy!" said Nikki.

"Oh! My bad. Well, howdy, Cowboy!" The pastor petted the kit with a finger. Patch leaned into it and I could have floated all the way to Heaven, I was so proud!

"Has he been staying at Marta's with his big brother?"

Nikki nodded. "Yeeeah." She was coming out of her jacket a little.

"How long has he been leash-trained?"

"This morning!"

"This morning! Get outta here!"

"I taught him! We used a whole bag of treats!"

"Well! He oughta be ready for the Pet Parade!"

This time both Nikki and JP spoke. "Pet Parade?"

"Yeah, I think it starts"—he checked his wrist—"a half-hour from now. I guess they're going to gather up all the pets who've come and have their owners walk them through the Winter Wonderland display. I'm not sure if there's a prize, but hey—couldn't hurt, right?"

JP's eyes glittered. "A prize...!"

"What?" said Marta, coming back from her father's side. She stuffed white tissue in her pocket and zipped it up.

"We're going to be in the Pet Parade," said JP. He asked the pastor, "Where is it?"

While he pulled out a piece of marked paper, I heard Marta say, "Baba, want to be in a parade?"

The hound bayed her happiness. "Land's sake, I'm gonna be in a Christmas parade with an angel, wearing my best sweater! Oh, and right after I done been to the groomer's, too! What a

132

grand day this is turnin' out to be!"

"What's a parade?" asked Patch.

"It's a thing humans do Outdoors. They do a big one on TV on Thanksgiving." I squinted, filing through my TV memories. "There are these things called balloons...and they fly down the road, but slowly...And on the ground, there are humans in the leftover costumes that weren't scary enough for Halloween."

"Balloons? Costumes?" Patch's eyes bugged out.

"Yeah! You're gonna be in a parade, Cowboy! But you can't ride Bronco. ...'cuz he's inna PURSE!" Nikki threw back her head and cackled.

Her mom looked at her in surprise, mouth starting to smile.

"Okay, okay, enough about Bronco's bag," said JP. "Come on, let's go!"

"All right," said Ms. Daly. "If you need me, call my cell. I agreed to help Mr. and Mrs. Rivera with their booth."

JP marched us down one of the roads. Baba kept pace with her long brown legs, which was helpful because JP was moving so fast that all the sights and scents around me blurred together into one big soup. Having the big dog there kept me steady.

At last, the roads opened up on a row of white scenery, small human buildings and candies, Christmas themes.

"Is that snow?" asked Patch, reaching a paw towards the scenery.

Baba gave a big sniff, then snorted. "No, young cat, that's just cotton and white paint."

JP stopped in front of a lady with a funny burgundy vest that went down to her knees. Seeing me, she cooed, "Hi, kitty!"

"Is this where you sign up for the Pet Parade?" he asked.

I kept an ear on them while I checked on Patch. Nikki was doing a good job cuddling him close, and even spoke into his ear.

"Not so close, Baba," said Marta, leaning back on the dog's leash.

"Humans," said Baba. "They bring you to such interesting-smelling places, then tell you to quit sniffin'. What's a poor dog to do?"

"Over here," said JP, then he trooped away from the snow-scene, Marta and Nikki following.

Christmas quilts had been hung up between some trees to form the wall of a fort. I smelled dogs behind them.

Before Nikki stepped behind the curtain, there was an explosion of woofs and barking.

"Hey! Who's out there? He's no dog!"

"I think it's a cat!"

"There's more than one!"

"What's cats doing here?"

"Gingersnap?" Patch's voice wavered. He dug his claws into Nikki's sweater. She crooned at him, but even my fur was fluffed. I couldn't let Patch get eaten by dogs when we were so close!

It was Baba who reassured us both.

"Set your worries down, you cats. Today you're part of MeMe's pack. Y'all hear that?" shouted the hound to the dogs as we stepped behind the quilt curtain. "These cats is my pack, so don't none of y'all go bothering them now!" She eyed every dog in turn: a brown Chihuahua like Sammy, wearing a red and green sweater; a square-bodied terrier who was jumping straight up and down; a black-furred retriever; and a stout but strong-bodied dog with a smushed face. They all leaned on their leashes towards me and Patch.

The jumping dog stopped, pink tongue lolling. The jingle bell collar he wore around his jangled to a halt. "Whaa, Baba? These really are cats? I never seen cats Outdoors before," he said.

"Least, not on a leash." The retriever rose up on two legs to sniff at Patch's jacket. My hackles bristled to see such a big strange dog next to the little kit, but Baba caught me and said, "It's OK, Sir Angel, I see these fellas on walks all the time. They're my neighbors—Riss-riss, you leave that kitten alone, you're raisin' his dander, see?'

"Sorry, said the black dog, and he went back on all fours.

"Angel," said the smush-faced dog. "I've been smelling angel around my house ever since my sister crossed the Rainbow Bridge," she said.

"That happens sometimes," said the Chihuahua. "They cross back to check on their families. Hey, Angel Cat, you looking after your fam?"

"No," I said. "Just helping this kit get to the family he needs to be in."

The Chihuahua's eyes bulged further out of his apple-shaped head. "You mean he doesn't have his Forever Home yet?"

"Forever Home?" said the smush-faced dog. "What's that?"

"Jenni's got a pedigree," said the Chihuahua to me. "Purebred English bulldog. Never lived in a shelter."

"I've never lived in a shelter," said Patch.

"No, sugartail, but you done lived Outdoors your whole life," said Baba. "Jenni was born Indoors, raised with humans and her dog family until she got big enough to go to her Forever Home. Isn't that so, Jenni?"

"Yes, MeMe. But my girls don't treat me fancy," said the bulldog, accepting a scritch from her human, a girl about the age of my Gina before I died. I wondered if she'd been at College, too.

"Your Christmas hoodie sure is fancy, Jenni," said Riss-riss.

The bulldog grinned. "Thanks, Riss-riss."

"Guys, you miss the point," said the Chihuahua. "It's Christmastime and he needs a Forever Home. Ping Pong, you remember your shelter, right?"

The terrier rolled on the grass. "Yep."

"Where would you rather be at Christmas? Your house, or your shelter?"

The terrier barked. "Good joke, Pinto Bean! I wouldn't go back to a shelter if you threatened to take away all my tennis balls!"

The retriever gasped. "All your tennis balls? Are shelters really that bad?"

"Yes," said the Chihuahua, stomping a tiny paw. He put his forepaws on Nikki's leg. "How can we help, *mijo*? Is there any way we can help you get your Forever Home?"

"Well…" Patch looked at me, but I just purred some encouragement. Sooner or later, he would have to figure out the things he needed without me.

"I want to get down and walk in the parade," said the kit. "Will you be nice to me when I'm on the ground?"

"Sure, man!" said the Chihuahua, and to my surprise, Baba's other dog friends joined in agreement.

"And MeMe will be right here by you, little one," said Baba. "No strange dog'll get a holda you while we're here!"

Patch took a breath, then began squirming down Nikki's arms.

"Cowboy! Do you wanna meet the doggies?" said Nikki. And then—*plop*—Patch was on the ground at her feet while Nikki held the end of his leash. The dogs rushed him, sniffing, but Baba blocked them with her be-sweatered body. "Now don't everybody crowd him! One at a time if you please."

While the dogs and Patch exchanged curious sniffs, JP said, "Nikki, is that a good idea? He's awful small…"

He's bigger than that Chihuahua!

I leapt off JP's shoulder to the ground and sat next to Patch. "Hey!" said JP.

Jenni's cold wet nose pressed into my neck and I jumped. She didn't notice, though. "Oh, yes, definitely angel," she said. "If you happen to see my sister up there, will you tell her 'hi' for me? Her name is Lula."

I smoothed my fur back down. "Er—sure!"

Above me, JP spoke. "Whoa. They're all acting…nice."

"Maybe they think he's a dog, 'cuz of the leash," said Marta. I laughed and Baba laughed with me.

"Imagine that! A dog who'd get a cat mixed up with a dog just 'cuz he had a leash on 'im! Even if my smeller was broke, I hope to howl I'd be able to tell a cat apart from a dog!"

The makeshift curtain lifted and in came a group of children with their dogs. One of them howled, "Cat!" and charged, but Riss-riss ran up to them, blocking their way. Baba started forward.

"I got this, Sir Angel. You stay with your kit while me and Pinto explain," said the hound over her shoulder before she hurried over to the new arrivals.

The children took one look at Patch and laughed in surprise.

One girl in a red yarn hat bent down, fending off her dog's attempts to lick her. "Is that a cat?"

"Yeeeah," said Nikki in her slow drawl. "His name's Cowboy."

One of the boys—the girl's brother, from the smell of him— wrinkled his nose at Nikki.

"What's wrong with her?" he said.

JP stiffened behind me, but suddenly, Marta was in front of the mean boy, her mittened fists clenched at her side.

"Nothing! You wanna make something of it?"

The boy stepped back, seemingly addled by this pink-jacketed girl staring him down.

Attagirl, Marta!

Nikki watched them, eyes wary. But then the sister said to her, "Can I pet him?"

Nikki saw the eager smile on the girl's face and brightened up. "Sure!"

The girl ran a soft-looking hand over Patch, sliding off the jacket, over his furry rump, and going up his tail without pulling it. Then she gave me a head pat, though I was too busy watching her brother to acknowledge it.

"Who's she to you?" the boy asked Marta, jutting his chin out.

"My friend!"

Marta must have won the chin jutting contest, because the boy turned away to one of the other children he had come in with. But his sister kept talking to Nikki, and Nikki's smile kept growing.

In time, more children and dogs of all sizes joined us behind the curtain, and more often than not, some of them stopped to ask Nikki about Patch and me, even if their eyes first said they noticed Nikki was different from them. And, of course, Baba and Pinto Bean the Chihuahua made sure the new dogs didn't get their tails twisted about Patch, though judging from the whispers of "An angel!" and some of the sniffing I was catching, I could have put an end to that pretty quick!

The lady in the funny burgundy vest came behind the curtain.

"OK, kids! The parade's starting! Line up, then just follow the red line on the ground until you get to the end."

The children shuffled their dogs around until a wobbly line had formed. JP scooped me up and I wiggled to get down until Patch meowed up at me.

"I'm fine, Gingersnap."

"We'll guard him, Angel," said Riss-riss. "We'll do a good job. All of us."

From JP's shoulder I could see all of Baba's dog friends. Pinto Bean led Riss-riss, just ahead of Patch in line, while Baba, Jenni the bulldog, and Ping Pong followed my kit. I purred. Who'd have thought dogs could be so nice to a kit they didn't even know?

"Thank you, everyone," I said.

"Well, it's Christmastime, you know," said Ping Pong.

Jenni snorted. "Yeah! Some Good Dogs we'd be if we didn't help out an angel—even if he is a cat!"

The dogs chuckled until Pinto Bean sniffed. "Time to go, guys!"

Riss-riss padded forward with his owner.

"Your turn, Nikki," said JP, and his sister walked ahead with Patch.

The red line led us to the pretend snow scene we'd seen earlier, the Winter Wonderland. Half of it was on our weak-paw side, the rest on our grooming-paw side. We walked in-between. There were no balloons in this parade, or dancers. But there were humans cheering and clicking their rectangles at us.

When Nikki and Patch walked on, you could hear squeals in the crowd.

"Look, she's walking a cat!"

"Look at his cute coat! It looks like a red bandana!"

"Mommy, can we get Maxine a coat?"

"He's got a kitty on his shoulder!"

Suddenly I remembered that I hadn't groomed my blaze at all in the past hour! If I wasn't careful, I'd turn into a dog.

"Aw, ain't that nice how they like our young cat, Jenni?"

"He's popular, MeMe. He's a Good Kitty," said the bulldog.

We turned around the bend in the fake snow scenery. There in front of the rectangle-holding crowd, I saw a very familiar face peeking out behind a very strange gray contraption, one that was all angles, like boxes melted together, except for a part he squinted through with one eye. He seemed to be aiming the machine at us as we walk.

I put my paws on top of JP's yellow-capped head.

"Dwight! DWIGHT! It's me, Gingersnap!" I called.

"Whoa, Bronco!" said JP. "Watch the hat!"

The crowd laughed.

"You know that guy?" Patch called up to me.

"Yes! He's an angel, too, my partner! DWIGHT!"

JP pulled me off his head and started stuffing me into the front of jacket.

Nikki laughed, but I kept calling until the bearded angel pulled his face away from the contraption. He gave me a thumbs-up, but then pointed to a tall brown woman next to him. She turned to move ahead of the parade, but Dwight caught her and whispered in her ear, pointing at me and Cowboy.

Seeing us, a look like she'd come across a forgotten treat flashed across her face, and she hurried even faster to beat the parade. Dwight followed her without hesitating.

Huh! I wonder what that was about.

"You cold, Bronco?" JP asked. "Is that what you were complaining about?"

I licked his hand in apology, and he carried me through the rest of the parade in his cozy jacket. The whole time, though, I kept an eye out for my fellow angel.

CHAPTER TWENTY

The fake scenery led out into a little circle of chocolate-smelling building-boxes. Dogs from the parade milled around with their owners, and humans were handing out steaming white cups of drink to all the different children.

Standing near the middle of the circle was Dwight. When he spotted me again, he tapped the woman with him on the shoulder and lifted his chin at us. The woman came straight for us, holding a black stick with a bulb at the end of it. I'd seen those before on TV...I thought the word was "microphone".

"Uh, JP?" said Nikki, as the woman and Dwight came over. She quickly bent down and picked up Patch, who had been talking with Baba.

"It's okay," Marta whispered back.

When the woman spoke, her head turned to Nikki, then JP. Dwight stood behind her, aiming the superbox on his shoulder at us.

"Hi, kids, I'm Lana Fitzgerald from Channel Three News. Did you guys know you had the only cats in the entire Pet Parade here at the Christmas Fair?"

JP's face twisted up. "Kiiiinda?" he said, looking at his sister. She giggled, and so did the microphone woman.

"We'd love to do a story on you two. You and your cats would be on TV."

"We don't get local TV," said JP, turning a little red.

Marta elbowed him. "You guys gotta, JP! It'd be so cool."

"What do you say?" said the microphone woman. After another glance at Nikki, JP took her hand. Then he nodded at the woman.

"Great." She put the microphone under her chin and spoke. "Lana Fitzgerald reporting at the Christmas Fair in Hillerman Memorial Park. I'm here speaking with two young Pet Parade participants and their unusual animals."

Patch reached for the microphone with a paw. "What's that?"

"Is that your name, little fella?" The microphone woman asked Patch, hearing his meow.

"No!" said Nikki. "It's Cowboy. And this is his brother, Bronco."

My ear turned at a guffaw coming from Dwight's direction, but when I looked, the face behind the shoulder contraption was suspiciously blank.

"How long have you owned them?" asked the microphone woman.

"Couple days," said Nikki. "My brother found them at school."

"On the way home from school," said JP. "With my friend Marta."

Marta waved, huge smile turning her eyes into squinty lines.

"I wanted to bring them home to help my sister."

"Help her how?"

JP squared his shoulders. "She...she was in an accident this year at a water park where we used to live. She used to be an honors student in high school, but she got brain damage because she was under the water too long before anyone found her. After we moved here, she didn't want to go to school anymore. Or make friends. But now that she has Cowboy, she's talked to lots of people, and come out to the fair, and it's only been two days since she met him."

"That sounds amazing!" said the microphone woman.

"Yeah, it is, but Mom says we can't keep them past Christmas."

"Why not?"

"I mean, she wants to! But we don't have an apartment yet."

"Or a job," said Nikki absent-mindedly, scratching Patch's ears.

"Yeah, Mom's still looking for one."

JP hugged me tight. I butted my head against the underside of his chin.

"Well, I'm glad you at least have your kitties to keep you and your sister company during the holiday," said the woman. "They looked wonderful in the parade."

Both Nikki and JP beamed up at her. But there was that hurt in his eyes again.

"Thanks!" said Nikki.

The woman turned to Dwight's contraption and said something, but I was busy purring for JP. *Everything will be OK.* Oh, how I wish I could talk to humans sometimes!

The woman turned back from Dwight and let the microphone stick relax at her side. "You two'd better go get some cocoa, it's free for anyone who was in the parade."

"Oooh!" said Nikki, and she and JP ran me and Patch towards the smell of chocolate. Over JP's shoulder, I watched Dwight put his contraption down and talk to Marta while the microphone lady listened.

The sound of claws clicking made me look down. Nikki had set Patch on the ground again and Baba's friends were gathering. Ping Pong the terrier's jingle bells rang as he jumped up and down at the end of his loose leash. His sentences came out in a rush between jumps. "Wow, pup!—I mean, kit!—You're gonna be —on TV!—Maybe you'll be—on the innertubes,—too!"

"It's called the 'interwebs', goofball," said Jenni the bulldog. "And it's way cool, Cowboy."

"Yeah, I'll look for you," said Riss-riss. "My mom always watches the news."

"Thanks, guys," said Patch.

"Good walking out there, everyone," said Pinto Bean. He was trembling, but not from cold. Sammy did it, too, in Heaven.

"Out of habit," he told me once.

But Patch noticed. "Pinto Bean, are you OK?"

"Oh, sure. Except I don't got no one to play Chase 'n' Dodge with!"

"Chase 'n' Dodge?"

"Yeah." The dog's bottom went up and he stretched his forelegs on the ground. "Wanna learn how to play?"

"OK," said Patch.

Marta and Baba walked up.

"What'd the cameraman ask you?" said JP.

Marta shrugged. "Wanted to hear my part of the story. No big. Did you get some cocoa?"

"Yeah. I wish the prize had been something else, though. I thought...maybe if I won some money, we could board the cats for a couple of nights."

"Hm. Yeah. That would've been good," said Marta, looking mournfully into her cocoa. But then the next minute, she jumped, sloshing cocoa on her mittens.

"Whoa, kitty!"

I looked down. The kit was bounding around with the Chihuahua. Incredible!

"Patch! You're playing with a dog!" I said.

"Uh-huh?" he said, keeping his eye on Pinto Bean.

"Patch, *I've* never played with a dog!"

"Really? It's kinda fun!" he said. He pounced on Pinto Bean.

Now Riss-riss bowed his front legs. "Can I play, too?"

"Sure!" said Pinto Bean and Patch.

Soon, all of Baba's dog friends were in the game. I watched Patch stalk and run and play with the huge dogs like they were his littermates. They were all being gentle with the kit, but I couldn't help but admire him.

"He's a Good Cat," said Baba. "And I hope he gets to stay with Marta's friends." She scratched the ground. "Sounds like they been having a bad year, from what Marta told your angel friend. Why, their daddy even left them after the girl's accident. And it sounds like Nikki was somethin' really special over at School before she drownded."

"She's still special," I said. Nikki hurried behind Patch with the leash, keeping him in the dogs' game.

The hound's droopy eyes widened. "You're right, Angel. My mouth was runnin' ahead of my brain, there. Forgive an old hound."

I gave her a slow blink. "Always."

"She's special, all right! They deserve a break this Christmas. If I could, I'd give 'em a real home where they could have a pack of cats if they wanted."

"Me, too, Baba. Me, too."

CHAPTER TWENTY-ONE

After the drive to Marta's house, JP and Nikki's mother came to visit us in the shed. It wasn't quite as dusty as before. If someone had pushed the awful vacuum cleaner around here, I was glad they'd decided to do it while we were gone!

After the game of Chase 'n' Dodge with the dogs, Patch had fallen asleep at the fair. Nikki had taken the pink jelly bag from JP and had carried the kit around in it for the rest of the day. But now that we were in the shed, he was awake, and the nap had fueled his kitten energy reserves. He skittered around the room, occasionally pouncing on me in the cat game we call "Death from Above", but to be honest, my heart wasn't in it.

"Mom, we were in the Pet Parade! I talked to so many kids —they said they wished they had a cat who could go outside on a leash. Mom, isn't that cool? Cowboy is so cool! You gotta let us keep him. Do you think I could take him with me to school? Next year? Maybe?"

"And Bronco, too," added JP. "Please? I could sell hot chocolate...or clean peoples' windshields or cars or something, and maybe I could raise the money to board them somewhere!"

Their mother didn't say anything for a while. Patch chomped on my head and tried to wrestle me, but I caught his head between both paws and hugged him to me. His feet battered against my blaze as he tried to get away, but I had him!

Nikki clapped. "Keep trying, Cowboy!"

"They're really good for Nikki, JP, you're right. But we just don't have any place to keep them. And boarding animals is expensive. Besides, Cousin Becca will be back tomorrow. I'm not sure you'd make enough money in time."

I let the kit go. He ran in circles around me until JP picked him up and began rubbing his tummy.

"We just don't have any place to keep them right now," their mother went on. "I'll try to call around—Marta's mom said she'd let me borrow her church directory—but a lot of people are out of town this time of year, or going out of town, like the Riveras. We may not be able to find someone, so please...keep your expectations realistic."

Marta spoke up. "Are you sure your Cousin Becca can't—"

"Uh-uh," said JP. "Mom said it's a no-pet zone. She gets too sick." He sighed.

"I know. I know," said Ms. Daly. "I really really hope we find someone to keep your kitties, guys, but I'm just not seeing how that's going to happen."

JP muttered something into Patch's fur that I didn't catch.

"What about Dad?" said Nikki.

"He's too far away now, honey. He couldn't drive down in time."

JP sunk his head on his knees, eyes angry. "Probably wouldn't even try," he said.

"JP." Ms. Daly's tone made Patch cower. "This is our life, now."

"Yes, Mom."

Ms. Daly ran her hand through her hair. "I can promise you I'll do everything I can do. I'll call through that church directory after work tomorrow. And when Cousin Becca gets back tomorrow, I'll talk to her, too."

"Really?" said JP.

"Really," she said. "Maybe she knows someone."

JP set Patch down. He started fighting my tail, so got up and I meandered over to Ms. Daly. She reached for me and I thought I might get a head rub, but she put her hand on her lap and pushed herself up, instead.

"Let's say goodbye to the Riveras. You can come back in the morning and play with the cats. The Riveras are being kind enough to host them until the day after Christmas, so be sure to thank them."

"We will," said all three children.

JP rubbed me tail-to-nose, then undid the damage, saying, "See you tomorrow, Bronco. Stay warm."

Then he stood. Meanwhile, Nikki cuddled Cowboy. She whispered something in his ear, then set him down. Then the Daly family and Marta left the shed, closing the door behind them.

Patch looked at the door.

"What'd she say to you?" I asked.

"Fuzzy Christmas Eve," he said. "Did you hear what JP said to me when he was holding me?"

I shook my head.

The kit fixed me with his blue eyes. "He said, 'It'll take a miracle.'"

I flicked my tail. "That's doable!"

Patch pounced on me. "You mean it?"

I licked his forehead. "I'm going to try. Watch my face, please."

He lowered himself to the ground, tail flipping in interest. "Okay."

I prayed the words with all my heart, knowing it was the right thing to ask for.

We need a miracle. The Dalys need a home by Christmas, or else Patch can't stay with them. Please send them a home!

I opened my eyes. "Has my face changed at all?" I hadn't felt a warm feeling, but maybe this miracle was different.

Patch frowned. "...Nooo."

Hm! "I'll try it again," I said.

I prayed again that Nikki's family would get a new home by Christmas. No warm feeling.

"How 'bout now? Anything change?"

"Nuh uh. What am I looking for, again?"

"There's a stripe on my face—my last miracle stripe. If I use my miracle, it will disappear."

He bobbed his head side to side. "Nope, all your stripes are still there."

I thought of where the bobtail had whacked me with her paw.

"It's around my eyes."

"Oh, it's THAT stripe? No, it's THERE, Gingersnap."

I lashed my tail. "I'll try a different prayer."

Please, if a new home is too much, too fast, just give them a place to keep Patch until they get a place of their own.

No warm feeling.

"It's still there, isn't it?"

He nodded.

I swallowed. Was I asking too much?

"Okay. I'll...I'll keep trying tonight. It's...it's a biggie." *Bigger than flying out from under a car and landing up a tree?* "Maybe it will take more time. You get some sleep. I'll keep praying for the miracle."

He wrapped his tail around him, troubled blue eyes avoiding my gaze. But soon he was snoring. I sat facing the window and prayed.

When the sun rose later, I pounced on the kit.

"Look at my face. Is the stripe gone?" I thought I'd felt a warm feeling, but then again, I also thought I might have dozed off once or twice during the night.

Bleary-eyed, he squinted at me. I stood mouse-still.

Patch looked down at the floor. "No," he said. "You look the same."

I sat back on my haunches.

How could it be? This was my mission—what He sent me down here for! I tried asking every way I knew how—I asked for a small miracle when I thought I was asking too much; I asked for a giant miracle when I thought I wasn't thinking BIG ENOUGH. Why wouldn't my request be granted?

"Gingersnap?" Patch said softly.

Maybe the fallen world was just too big for one cat—even an angel cat—to make a difference.

"Gingersnap?"

Or maybe it was too late? Had the snow come early? I leapt to the windowsill, but the yard was bare of snow.

"Gingersnap? Couldn't it still happen?"

I looked over the yard one more time, but though the fruit-colors of the lights gleamed in the window's reflection, not a speck of white snow shone anywhere, not in the grass or on the wall or atop the trees...

Tiny claws swiped my dangling tail.

"Gingersnap!"

I leapt back down to the floor.

"How could this happen? We did everything right. She loves you! You learned to walk on a leash for her! And now..." I looked at the kit. "That's it?"

The kit came up to me, pulled my head aside with a paw, and began licking my ears.

I sighed. He groomed me, purring the whole time. It was a while before I could lift up my head.

"Sorry, kit. I'm supposed to be the angel here." I gave him an apologetic lick. "What was it you were saying?"

"I asked, couldn't it still happen? I mean, they just have to find a place for me for a little while. And Nikki's mom will be calling people today. Maybe it'll just...you know...happen."

My tail swished. "That's...not a bad notion, kit!"

His tail lifted. "Yeah?"

"Yeah! All miracles are good things, but not all good things have to be miracles." I started to chirrup my joy, but wound up yawning, instead.

"You were up all night, huh? Why not catch a few winks before Nikki and her family get here? If your face changes, I'll tell you."

"Tha"—I yawned again—"anks." I curled up next to him. "Don't mind if I do."

CHAPTER TWENTY-TWO

The children came later that morning. While JP cleaned our litter, Marta plugged in a little heating box her mom had given her. Afterwards, the children talked quietly about Christmas and gifts and the movies while they played with Patch and me. JP even brought a board game so Patch could chase dice.

Mrs. Rivera brought out lunch for them, and later, when it was growing dim again, she brought them dinner.

They were just finishing when the door opened with its familiar creak. The children hushed immediately, JP's hand stopping on my head. Nikki hugged Patch closer.

JP and Nikki's mother entered first. Marta's mother came after her, closing the shed door behind her. She stayed there while JP and Nikki's mother sat on the Easter tub.

My heart thudded in my chest. Patch looked at me; I saw the way his eyes traveled across my face, looking at the miracle that hadn't worked.

Please no, Lord. Nikki and Patch need each other. What kind of Christmas memory will it be if she has to give him up tomorrow?

"Cousin Becca and her husband came home," said Ms. Daly. "I explained everything to them. They said they're very sorry, and understand and love how much Cowboy and Bronco have helped us this past week. But they've sold the motorhome to a couple who are as allergic to cats as they are."

Marta's face pinched, turning red with tears, but she made no sound.

"It was a great deal, they couldn't pass it up, and I don't blame them. The new owners will be picking up the motorhome in a few days. After Christmas, kids, we'll be moving into Cousin Becca's spare room."

Marta fled to her mother, who wrapped her in her arms.

Plunk. One of JP's tears fell into my fur.

"So...we have to take 'em to a shelter?"

"I'm sorry, honey." JP's mother swallowed hard and was silent again for a long time. "Even if Cousin Becca didn't get sick from them, we can't afford two extra mouths to feed right now."

JP leaned over, pulling his sister into a hug. His shoulders shook as he tried to cry silently, but little sobs escaped him. I lay my head on his lap. Nikki frowned down at nothing. Patch mewed, unsure.

Nikki had gone from hiding in her house to meeting with the Riveras every day, even going to the Christmas fair with her brother and Marta. She even spoke to strangers! But it looked to me like she was already retreating. Patch was good for her. And I knew she was good for Patch. But the miracle hadn't happened; I'd failed my mission, and now Patch would be in a shelter for who knows how long. And Nikki...well, I didn't know what would happen to her.

"We'll make sure it's a no-kill shel—shelter." Ms. Daly's voice caught. She took a deep, deep breath before continuing. "And we won't take them until the day after Christmas."

Nikki kept frowning and rubbing Patch's fur.

Ms. Daly swallowed hard. "I promise, once I get a job, once we can move out, we'll get you a new cat. We should be able to afford one."

"But it won't be Cowboy and Bronco, Mom," said Nikki. Then she burst into tears. Patch purred desperately as she wept into his fur.

Ms. Daly went to her children and knelt on the dusty carpet. She gathered us up in her arms.

"I'm sorry, my loves. I wish things were different."

Her voice was strong, but from where I lay, I could see the two tears running down Ms. Daly's face. "I wish I could make things different for all of us. But we're going to get through this."

She sniffed. JP looked up, startled. Seeing the tears on his mother's face, his face crumpled again, and his mother stroked his cheek with her palm. Nikki looked up, eyes sharp like claws until she, too, saw her mother's tears. Her face softened, and she lay her head on her mother's shoulder.

"I know you love these cats, munchkins. But even if Marta wasn't going away for so long, they can't live in a shed all their lives. They deserve better."

"Mom?" said Nikki. Her voice was warbly from crying.

"Yes, Pumpernickel?"

"Can me and JP sleep here tonight?"

Ms. Daly jolted upright.

I put my paw on her lap. "Please?" I asked.

Ms. Daly turned to Marta's mother. Marta was hugged against her side, eyes bleary, but dry.

"I can't see why not," said Mrs. Rivera. "Do you kids have sleeping bags?"

"They do," said their mother. "I can go get them. Nikki, will you be warm enough with the heater?"

"We have extra blankets," said Mrs. Rivera quickly. "I'm sure they'll be fine. Marta can sleep in the house, if you think that would be more appropriate."

Marta gave her mother a confused look that she ignored.

"I'm okay with it this once, if you're comfortable with it."

"He's a sweet boy," said Mrs. Rivera. "I'm sure there won't be any trouble. And it'll make carpooling to the pastor's house easier."

At that, JP stood up, gathering me in his arms. What a shame to split us up just as he was getting good at picking up cats!

159

"No, Mom. I'll go home with you." He went over to Marta. "Take Bronco," he said.

She held her arms out for me. Before he handed me over, he whispered in my ear. "Sorry, Bronc. But I don't want Mom to be alone on Christmas Eve. I'll see you tomorrow."

He kissed me on the head and went over to his Mom. He offered her his hand. She seemed startled, then sniffed another tear, letting him help her up.

"Let's go get Nikki's sleeping bag," he said.

"Good idea," she said.

They came back some minutes later and laid out a pink and black sleeping bag next to the strawberry-looking bag Marta had brought in from the house. I lay on Marta's feet at the end of her bag, where the hot water bottle was.

Ms. Daly tucked in Nikki while Marta and I watched from our sleeping bag. JP leaned against the shed door.

"Mrs. Rivera said you can use the shower inside in the morning," Ms. Daly said to Nikki. "I'll be back at ten thirty to pick you up for Christmas at Pastor Wade's house. Marta, can you help Nikki with the time?"

"Yes, Ms. Daly."

"You're a good friend, Marta."

Marta smiled, just with her mouth.

Ms. Daly turned to leave.

"Ms. Daly?" said Marta.

She turned back. "Yes, Marta?"

"Merry Christmas," she said.

"Yeah, Mom. Merry Christmas," said Nikki softly.

Ms. Daly smiled, a sad, proud, soft smile. "Merry Christmas, girls," she said.

"Merry Christmas, Marta. Merry Christmas, sis," said JP. His hand twisted the doorknob, but Nikki shouted. "Wait a minute, footface!"

"What?!" he said.

She held up Patch with one hand. "You didn't say Merry Christmas to the kitties!"

"Yeah!" said Marta. "Remember the kitties!" She wiggled her feet beneath me. The water bottle sloshed.

JP grinned. "Merry Catsmas, Bronco. Merry Catsmas, Cowboy. I'll make sure Santa brings you some tuna tomorrow."

Nikki covered Patch's ears. "John Paul! You're not supposed to spoil their Santa surprise!"

"C'mon. We better go so Santa can come," said Ms. Daly. "Love you," she said. They opened the door and went out into the cold night.

It was Christmas and the snow would come tomorrow. I could feel it in my whiskers.

What does this mean? What will happen to Nikki and Patch? JP and Marta?

I pondered these things while the girls chattered. Finally, Marta scampered out of her sleeping bag and, running over in her slippers, shut off the shed light. Now there was only the glow of the Christmas lights outside, and the heater.

"Nikki?" said Marta.

"Yeah?" Patch got to be under the covers with Nikki; right now she rubbed his chin with her finger while he drooled.

"I know after tomorrow there won't be a reason for you to come by. But do you think I could visit you sometimes? I...I think you're neat."

The dim light caught Nikki's bright teeth and pink gums as a smile lit up her face. "Yeeah. You're nice, Marta."

"Thanks, Nikki. Well...goodnight, I guess. And Fuzzy Christmas."

"Fuzzy Christmas to you, too."

Marta turned over and was soon snoring. Nikki spent a lot of time looking at Patch and rubbing the gray fur on his head, but finally her eyes closed and her breathing grew steady with sleep. Patch's eyes still glinted in the Christmas lights. Carefully, I stepped off Marta's hot water bottle and went to him.

"One more day," he said. "Then I'm in a shelter, I guess."

I held my tail tip against him, careful not to tickle Nikki.

"Shelters aren't the end of everything, Patch. You'll find a great family, I'm sure, just like how I found my Damien."

"Yeah, but..." he glanced at the girl cuddling him in her sleep. "I don't think I'll ever get this again, will I?"

I sighed. "I don't know, kit. I sure hope you do. But I don't know."

We didn't say anything a while. The heater box came on with a wooshy sound and a glow, then went dark again.

"Gingersnap?" said Patch.

"Yes, Patch?"

"I'll miss you," he said. "I'm glad you were my angel. I'm sorry the miracle didn't happen."

I gave him careful licks on his face. "So am I."

He put his paw on mine. "But you did a great job, OK?"

"We both did, kit. We both tried our best, but...sometimes this fallen world is bigger than us alley cats."

"But we tried," he said, jutting his jaw out.

"We did," I agreed.

We touched noses in the silence. For a while, we listened to the girls' breathing. But after a while, I stretched, ready to go back to Marta's sleeping bag when Patch touched his paw to mine again. "Gingersnap? Give me more tips? For the shelter?"

I stopped and turned around.

I stood there, smelling the less-dusty shed, feeling the coming snowfall in my whiskers, seeing the face of this young cat peeping out from under the chin of the sleeping girl, the girl who'd had an accident that had changed everything for her family but who looked perfect and peaceful when she slept, and I said, "No. No shelter tips tonight. But how 'bout a story?"

"Sure!"

I lay down, tucking my paws beneath me.

"I guess I shouldn't call it a story. It really happened. And because it did, we can look forward out of our dark and sad days and know that everything will be all right. And we can know that, as bad as things get, we're never alone.

"It happened many years ago, in a dry and dusty land far away. A human woman had to have her baby in a manger in a stable. But this was no ordinary baby, for He was the King of All, of both humans and us beasts...and yet He loved us all enough to come down as a little baby, so He could save us, and the world we live in, and the people we love..."

CHAPTER TWENTY-THREE

My whiskers seemed to burn the next morning awaiting the inevitable snowfall. They ached while my bones sang in the knowledge that all animals had, that this was Christmas Day, the celebration of the Lord's birthday. The sensations were enough to drive a squirrel crazy, so while Mrs. Rivera got the girls ready, I clung to Marta's sleeping bag.

Patch came over. "Your nose is quivering. You feel it too?" he asked. I just nodded.

Finally, the girls came to put us in the car. I hardly heard their talking, but jolted to when I realized Baba wasn't walking with us.

"Where's MeMe?" I asked Patch. "Do you know? Isn't she coming?"

"I heard Marta say her arthritis is acting up. She has to stay home where it's warm."

I sighed again. That old hound would know the right things to say today.

The window rolled down and I startled. Ms. Daly was in the car, but so was a man!

"Uncle...Uncle Dave!" said Nikki.

"He came down as a surprise," said Ms. Daly.

"Hiya, Tricky-Nikki!" said the man. "Who you got there?" He pointed to Patch.

"Cowboy," she said.

"And this one's Bronco," said Marta, lifting me up a little.

"They're staying with us. But just for Christmas," said Ms. Daly, beaming a meaningful stare around to each of the children, but lingering on JP. Maybe there was another reason he had gone home with his mother last night!

"Oh, okay! Christmas boarders! Hurry, come in, I can see your breath!"

Inside the car, Marta unzipped me from inside her pink jacket where she'd been carrying me and handed me over to JP. He zipped me up in his red jacket. He wore a Santa hat today, with a white puffball flopping around the end of it. Those puffballs were my guilty Christmas pleasure to play with, but all it did now was make me heave a sigh.

I watched Marta help buckle Nikki in next to us. Patch was in her arms, wearing his red walking jacket and leash, but the pink jelly bag sat at her feet.

166

Marta shut the door without slamming it. She was a nice girl, already wise to us cats. I was going to miss her.

"Is Aunt...Aunt...Is she here, too?" asked Nikki.

"Sure is," said the man, Uncle Dave. "She had a last-minute assignment she had to upload, so she'll be meeting up with us at the pastor's place later."

A car beetled out around us, made a goose sound.

"There's your mom, Marta."

Our car began to follow the other one. Patch gave an unsure mew.

"Aw, it's okay, little guy," said Uncle Dave.

I just squeezed tighter to JP, watching out the window. My whiskers were still tingly.

Oh, come on with it. I already failed Patch. You may as well come, snow.

But there wasn't a flake in the sky when the children clumped out of the car onto the pastor's lawn. No matter where I looked in the bleary sky, there was no motion, nothing white drifting down.

"You looking for Santa, buddy?" JP asked me.

"Maybe he's going to eat a...a snowflake on his tongue!" said Nikki.

Marta rang the bell.

"I didn't think it snowed here," said Uncle Dave.

"If it does, it'll be a miracle," said Mrs. Rivera. "It's been two years since the last snowfall, and it didn't stick." Next to her, Mr. Rivera nodded.

The door opened. Pastor Wade gave us a great smile. Behind him I could smell turkey, ham, and other good foods hanging in the air.

"Merry Christmas, guys! Come in, come in! I haven't seen it this cold in a coon's age!"

"I hope it's all right...the cats..." said Ms. Daly.

"You know what? That's just fine, we know they're special cats."

Dave shook the pastor's hand. "Thanks for having us on such short notice."

"Hey, what's Christmas all about? I can't tell you there's no room in this inn. Is your wife coming?"

"She'll be along."

The pastor gave two thumbs up. "Perfect. Come on in, my wife's just pulling the breakfast casseroles out, we'll bless the food, then eat."

The dinner table in the pastor's house was huge, and other tables were set up too, all with humans at them: some young, some old, some alone, some in pairs. At one table sat four children with hair so yellow it was almost white, just like the pastor's. A Christmas tree stood in the corner, twinkling colors like flowers. It was a smaller —much smaller—tree than I'd decorated at Cleanwhisker Farm, but there were dozens and dozens of shiny-wrapped present boxes piled around it. Oh, how I'd miss being down here!

"Ms. Daly, Nikki, JP, we saved you a spot here at the big table."

Patch leaned off Nikki a little, sniffing at the good smells coming from the table.

Marta took a place between her mother and father at a table near the fireplace.

"Oh, and Ms. Daly?" said the pastor. "Are you still moving after Christmas?"

"Yes, Pastor."

"I hope this isn't forward, but I told a few of our parishioners, and I've got a few families lined up who'd be happy to help you move."

Ms. Daly looked down. "It's just a few feet...from an RV into the house..."

"Still. The offer's there." He squeezed her shoulder.

"Thank you, Pastor."

"No problem."

Just then, the pastor's wife came out from the kitchen wearing red and green mitts and carrying a big pan of something flaky-smelling. She set it on the main table, then raised her voice.

"OK, everyone! Let's have the blessing, then we can start." The humans began holding one another's hands. JP scooched me to one arm and put his hand on his sister's shoulder. The human woman on his other side did the same, her hand frail and shaking. I licked it and she chuckled in her wizened voice.

"Honey?" The pastor's wife turned to her husband.

His smile turned thoughtful. "You know what? I got a feeling we should mix it up this year. JP?"

The boy squeezed me tight. "Yes, sir?"

"Could you give us the prayer?"

Ms. Daly looked at her soon, worry lines under her eyes.

"I've never done it before," he said.

"You don't have to if you don't want to," said the pastor.

"No...I'll...I'll try."

The pastor's smile was like a sun. "Just speak from the heart. You'll do great."

JP took a deep breath. I purred. The old woman next to us squeezed his shoulder. JP bowed his head and closed his eyes, just like the other humans.

"Um, God? We're here. We're thankful for Pastor Wade, the food, and that it's Christmas. Um..." There was a long pause. The youngest of the straw-blonde children opened one eye. I stuck my tongue out at her, and she giggled.

"Thank you for our families and friends and pets..." another long pause. "...and we hope you're having a good Christmas up there, too. Um...that's it," he ended in a whisper.

Amen, I thought.

"Amen," said the pastor.

"Amen," said everyone else.

But before we could even sit down, the doorbell rang.

The pastor jumped away from his chair and went to the door.

"Go ahead and start without him," his wife told the room.

"Go ahead and start without me," her mate called a second later.

She smiled. "This is our normal."

JP was passing a basket of rolls to the old woman when the pastor ducked his head back in.

"Ms. Daly? You're needed outside. JP? Nikki? Marta? You guys, too."

Frowns passed between the children and their mother. JP pushed us away from the table. Uncle Dave stood to come, but Ms. Daly waved him back down. She had both hands on her children's shoulders when we all stepped outside.

"Dwight!" I called when I saw him. His grey superbox was up by his face, his smile broad between his dark beard. The microphone woman had her microphone in one hand and a big blank cardboard rectangle in her other hand, bigger than two pizza boxes, at least!

"Hey, JP! Hey, Nikki! Hey, kitties!" said the microphone woman.

JP ducked, suddenly shy.

"Are you Christine Daly?" asked the woman.

"Yes," she said. She glanced at Dwight's superbox. "What's wrong?"

"I'm Lana Fitzgerald from Channel Three news. We spoke to your children at the Christmas Fair this past week."

She hugged her children in tight. "Uh huh?"

"They explained your situation to us—about your tough year, being new in town, and just wanting a place of their own so they can keep their cats, which you son says are really helping your daughter recover from her accident."

"Yes...?" Ms. Daly looked like she was waiting for a cage door to slam shut. But kindness was in the microphone woman's smile.

"Well...the segment was archived on our online video page. A young girl by the name of Cassidy saw it and wanted to help. She has a service animal, too, and knows how important they are to their owners. With the help of her parents, she started a Gener-US-ity campaign on behalf of your family. We announced this development to our viewers in a follow-up video."

"...Yes?" Ms. Daly looked confused as a kitten in a hole.

"There was a huge response from our community and organizations within our community."

JP and Marta looked at each other.

Ms. Daly's eyes were bulging now. "YES?! And??"

The woman turned the big white cardboard around. "On behalf of News Three and our community of viewers, I'd like to present you with this check for thirty-five thousand dollars."

Nobody moved for a second. And then Ms. Daly fell down.

"MOM?" yelled JP, dropping to his knees. Ms. Daly's face was buried in her hands. I could smell the tears from here.

"Mom?" said Nikki, softly. "Why are you crying?"

Ms. Daly sobbed a little more, then finally looked up, smile twisting out of the tears.

"B...because...you can keep your cats now."

"REALLY?!" shouted Nikki, clutching Patch.

Marta grabbed JP and jumped for joy. "JP!"

He jumped with her. I bobbed up and down with each rebound, in a daze. I still couldn't believe my ears. Patch was going to stay with Nikki. And the snow hadn't fallen! I hadn't failed my mission! He was going home with Nikki!

"Should be more than enough to get you guys in a nice big apartment," said Dwight. "Miss Lana, why don't you tell her the rest?"

"There's more?" squeaked Ms. Daly.

"As a result of the Gener-US-ity campaign, some local businesses took a look at your online resume. Four of them would like to interview you, but you'll be able to choose which position you go with. All of them said from the look of your qualifications, they'd be happy to have you."

Tears rolled down Ms. Daly's face. "Thank you. Thank you."

"Here, Mom." Nikki stuck Cowboy in her mother's face. "Cowboy will help you feel better."

Ms. Daly took Patch. He began licking away her tears, and finally she laughed.

"Thank you. Thank you. You're all angels. Merry Christmas!" She hugged the kit to her.

Then she looked up at the pastor. "Looks like we're going to need help moving after all."

He laughed. Patch's new family all laughed with him.

I looked upward toward Heaven. *Thank You, Lord.*

The first snowflake drifted down. I reached for it.

* * *

We went back inside, where Pastor Wade explained what had gone on Outdoors. It had been a surprise to him, too. The snow was falling nonstop now, white fluff like a summer

173

shedding. JP and I had no sooner sat down when the doorbell rang for the second time. Pastor Wade jumped up again.

"That'd better not be for me," said Ms. Daly. "If I cry anymore, I'll dry up into an old husk."

"Or jerky!" said JP.

"Or a...mummy!" said Nikki.

Uncle Dave smiled. "After what you've been through this year, sis, I'm surprised you haven't cried yourself into a puddle."

"You're absolutely right."

"What's this about a puddle?" said a familiar voice.

I looked up.

No...it couldn't be!

The children jumped up.

"Aunt Gina! Aunt Gina!"

She hugged us all. She was a little older now, but I'd never forget her voice, her scent, the way her arms wrapped around a body.

"And who's this handsome boy?" she asked Nikki, pointing to Patch.

"Cowboy," said Nikki, grinning. "My cat."

"Well hello, Cowboy, Nikki's cat."

Gina offered her fist to the kit and he rubbed his head against it.

That's my girl.

"Is this *your* Gina?" whispered Patch. "The baby?"

"Sure is," I said.

Then she turned to JP and me.

OK, I couldn't help it. I started talking a mile a minute.

"Oh my gosh," Gina said. "You're Mr. Chatty, aren't you?" She bent low to be face to face with me. Our eyes met, and she gasped in surprise.

I reached for her face with my paw. "Gina! It's so good to see you!" I said. "I missed you!"

"Whoa, boy!" said JP, trying to keep me from climbing onto her. "Sorry, he's usually really chill."

I tried touching noses with her. Our eyes filled each other's.

"What is it, Aunt Gina?" asked Nikki.

"He looks just like Gingersnap Cat—my cat we had growing up...The only thing different is this little mask he's got." She reached her finger towards my brow, but when her finger got in range, I kissed it instead. Pain came into her smile. "And of course, Gingersnap died years ago. He was an old man by then! Almost made it to twenty. I practically grew up with him. Hi, sweetheart," she said, plucking me out of JP's arms. "Are you a bandit?" she crooned in that voice I loved. "Are you a tuna bandito?" She cuddled me to her.

"His name is Bronco."

She frowned, mock-solemn. "That's a good name, Mr. Bronco-Bandito. I hope you've been a nice kitty to my nephew."

"Yes! They're my family, too! We're all family!"

She touched noses with me.

The snow went on, and the eating went on, and presents were opened, but I stayed with Gina, heart glowing, feeling like we'd never been separated by anything at all!

CHAPTER TWENTY-FOUR

I sat in the snow, admiring the smooth blanket left behind after the gray sky had moved on. It covered the pines and sticks that backed the pastor's yard, trailing off into a thin forest. Beyond that I could smell a crystalline blanket—maybe a field?

My ears caught the sound of that one song the humans always played at Christmas time. *I'm dreaming of a white Christmas.* I always wondered why they played that. *Christmases aren't white; they're full of reds and greens and golds.* Then I thought about the Christmases I'd seen in Heaven, all the humans running around wearing white, happy and together in the soft, smooth clouds.

Maybe they mean a pure Christmas. A peaceful Christmas. Humans get stuff like that wrong all the time.

Around the corner from me, the children scuffled and squeaked and rolled up balls of the white stuff to decorate.

I'd had enough goodbyes in my life to know I didn't like them. So when Gina had set me down after a long visit on her lap, I made sure to stay hidden, except to wish Patch luck.

"I gotta go, kit," I'd told him in private, hiding on the dining room seats that had been pushed beneath the table. I looked at him one last time, lining up this young feline before me with the first time I'd seen him in the cage, small and frightened. Now he could trust humans, walk with dogs—and maybe even go to school! "I'm proud of you, kit. I'll miss you."

"Thanks, Gingersnap. I'll miss you, too."

And that was that. He knew I knew he'd watch over the Dalys—and my Gina, too, if she came around. Keeping an eye on things is what we cats do, after all.

I took another breath of cold air. I could feel the call in my heart: time to go back home to Heaven. Patch was with his family, and they all would make a good home here together with their new friends, like Marta's family and the pastor's.

A light like a shooting star broke across the sky. My ride.

"Gingersnap? Partner?" My ears pricked. I couldn't see Dwight, but I knew it was him. I scented the air. He was in the distance, in the field past the forest. *"Time to go!"*

I stood, stretched, then made my way forward in the snow. I paused at the edge of the trees, considering one last deep claw sharpening before I went back to where trees weren't quite so satisfyingly solid when I heard JP behind me.

"Bronco?"

He stood alone at the corner of the house.

My purr dried up in my throat. I didn't mean for him to see!

I bounded towards the forest, but stopped when I heard his shoes crunching in the snow.

"Bronco!"

I turned around, facing him with my tail low. Even from here I could see the confusion on his face.

He thinks I'm running away.

"C'mon, boy. Let's go in for cocoa." He patted his chest, as if to urge me back into the front of his jacket. When I didn't come, he took a step forward. I took one back.

His voice quieted. "Bronco?"

I know he loves me, but I can't stay with him. This isn't what I want. If only I could tell him—

My miracle. I blinked my eyes. Gina said it was like I was wearing a mask.

Lord, please show him, and let him understand.

The warm-hug feeling spread from my tummy up my neck, 'til it reached the last miracle stripe. Funny, now my face felt cooler, like a mask *had* been lifted off.

"Bronco? What happened to your..." JP stopped. For a second, it looked like he was listening to something.

Then, understanding, like brightness, came over his face. He came forward again, but I didn't move any.

"You're an angel?" he asked me.

I slow blinked.

"You're...Aunt Gina's cat? Gingersnap?"

I slow blinked again.

"Wow," he said softly.

Then, slowly, he knelt and moved his hands towards me to scoop me up.

I trotted to him. He picked me up and hugged me tight. "Thank you for bringing Cowboy to us. I promise we'll take good care of him."

I purred and groomed his hair. He gave me a final kiss on my nose then set me back down.

"Thank you," he told me. Then he looked up to Heaven, smiling. He jumped up and down. "Thank You!" he shouted.

I spun around in a happy circle, joining his joy. When he was done, I rubbed against his ankles one final time, then ran into the woods.

As far as goodbyes went, it wasn't so bad.

CHAPTER TWENTY-FIVE

Dwight and I rode the red chariot up, up, past the darkening night of Earth to the moon-bright firmament of Heaven. We slowed to a stop a few hills away from the Cleanwhisker Christmas tree. A great gathering of cats surrounded the tree—cats spilling out of the barn hayloft, cats chatting by the tables of grass, cats dancing around the tree.

"Guess this is your stop, partner. Nice work."

"Thanks!" I said, climbing out of the pouch. The grass rustled under my paws with my landing. The feeling of absolute solidity had gone, but it wasn't bad, just different.

"Thanks for taking care of the human side of the mission," I told him. "Patch—I mean, Cowboy—wouldn't have made it without you."

"Just doing my job." He smiled. "That family needed a cat angel as much they needed a human one. I mean, if you two hadn't been the only cats at the fair, no one would have heard of your story. That story is what touched people's hearts—and people's hearts are where the miracles *really* happen. Anyway. Enjoy what's left of your Christmas, *Bronco*," he said with a wink.

Oh, humans!

"You too, Dwight. Merry Christmas."

"Merry Christmas." The chariot began to rise into the air again. Dwight sighed. "Time for the big family sing-along, I guess," he said, and then the chariot zipped away, turning into a whisker of light zooming towards the Human development. I watched it 'til it disappeared, then turned towards the glow of Cleanwhisker Barn's tree, ready to join the Christmas Rally.

But instead of the distant lions and lambs Christmas tree, I found the Lord's feet in front of me!

I bowed quickly. "Happy Birthday, my Lord!"

He grinned and threw his arms open. "Come here, Gingersnap!"

I couldn't resist the happiness in His voice. I leapt straight up in the air and He caught me in a hug.

"Well done, thou good and faithful servant!"

"Really, Lord?"

"Of course!"

"Did I do better than a dog?"

He laughed. "Oh, Gingersnap Cat! You served others in the best way you knew how, without thinking of a reward, and that makes it one of the best birthday gifts I can ever receive."

I purred.

"I'll be by later to celebrate with you and your friends. But I wanted to make sure you knew how pleased I was. It's not easy being an angel, is it?"

I thought for a second.

"Sometimes it is and sometimes it isn't."

"A very feline answer."

"But...it sure felt good knowing that I could help Patch because of all the things I'd lived through before. Good and bad." I touched the wound on the back of His palm. "But I guess You already know what that's like."

He kissed me between my ears. "Your friends have missed you." He lowered me to the hill. "Why don't you go join them?"

"I will. And Lord?"

"Yes, Gingersnap?"

"Thank You. For everything." It had been tough, but looking back, it had been wonderful. I'd helped a fellow cat in need, helped a human family, and gotten to see Gina again. And, best of all, the hole in me was gone. I didn't feel like a missing piece.

And even if that feeling came back, I'd know what to do about it.

"You're welcome," He said. "Now you'd better hurry. Those Christmas treats aren't going to eat themselves."

I slow blinked at Him, then dashed down the hill towards the Rally.

I hadn't touched the top of the hill in front of the tree when I was pounced upon.

"GIIIIN-GIEEEEE!" squealed Rodney in my ear.

I flipped him over my head with my back feet.

"Rodney! I missed you!" And I meant it. Wow!

We wrestled for a while until a new voice joined us.

"Gingersnap?"

"George!" I hopped off Rodney to greet the barrel-bodied cat. He raced over to touch noses with me. He let go of the catnip-scented sock in his mouth.

"How was angel-ing? It go well?"

"Tell us about it!" said Rodney.

"Tell, tell!"

Some of the clowder had split off to surround me. Even a few yet-to-be-born kittens stopped running up the tree to come see what the fuss was about.

I looked at their expectant eyes. "So much for a quiet Christmas recovery nap!" I said, and they laughed.

"For those of you who don't know me, my name is Gingersnap. I used to live on Earth with my family, but like all animals do, I got old and died. I live in Heaven now..."

* * *

"Brrr!" said Rodney when I was done. "I loved being alive, don't get me wrong, but I do NOT miss being cold."

George grinned. "I bet you looked funny with those miracle stripes!"

Rodney tittered. "He did!"

I shoved a paw in his face.

"Would you do it again?" called a somehow familiar voice from out of the clowder. I sat up on my haunches to see the bobtail cat smiling at me.

"You know," I said, watching the kittens snooze, "I think I would!"

AFTERWORD: THE REAL GINGERSNAP CAT

Years before my husband and I met, he was faced with the most difficult challenge of his life when unexplained health problems began ending his much-loved career. But before his employers could separate him from his post, he was stuck in a bureaucratic limbo, waiting for an official decision about his fate.

During this time he lived in an apartment complex, in a unit with a ground level door that opened onto some stairs. These stairs led into the living area of his second-story apartment.

It was on these stairs that he began making friends with two stray cats who hung around the complex. He started by leaving food and water out for them. He would leave his door open and sit on the steps, watching them and enjoying their company. As they became used to him, they began coming closer and closer, allowing him to pet them, until finally they came inside one day, as if to say, "OK, we're home."

They were both orange toms. My husband named the smaller one Pixel—after the titular cat from Robert A. Heinlein's novel *The Cat Who Walks Through Walls*—and the bigger one Gingersnap Cat.

Since I never knew Gingersnap, I asked my husband to describe him to me for the story. He was apparently stoic, and a little older than Pixel, who was something like a teen kitten at this time.

Finally the day came when my husband had to move out of his apartment. During this time, both cats had been confined to a room with their litterbox...until one of the movers accidentally opened the door. Pixel stayed inside, but Gingersnap escaped out the front door before anyone could catch him. My husband returned to the complex several times after the move, hoping to bring his second ginger friend with him, but my husband never saw the cat again.

So although Pixel is living a fine life with me and my husband these days (so spoiled he even has a publishing company named after him, natch), the mystery of what happened to Gingersnap still weighs heavily on my husband's heart.

The years between adopting Pixel and meeting me were hard on my husband. Oftentimes this little orange cat with white socks and mittens was the only thing getting him through some very hard times.

Knowing this, I suggested to my husband that Gingersnap may have been Pixel's kitty guardian angel, sent to make sure he got to the right home at the right time so he could see my husband through those rough years.

This book is a tribute to that idea—and to the memory of the real Gingersnap Cat. Wherever he is, we hope he's happy. The cat he left with us, Pixel, surely has been a major blessing in our lives.

Danielle Williams and Husband

Pictured: Pixel J. Cat, Esq.

SPECIAL THANKS

...to Brooke D., for checking the story for typos.

...to Joan B., for picking up typo duty when Brooke couldn't finish.

...to Sally J., for typo-checking the print edition.

...to Marisol T., for the shooting star transportation idea.

...to Joe W., for the great name "Riss-riss".

...to the Way of Cats blog (*www.wayofcats.com*), for posting such great information about cat personalities of all kinds.

...to my husband, for encouraging me during such a long project.

ABOUT THE AUTHOR

Danielle Williams has always loved talking animal stories. Some of her favorites include *Watership Down*, the *Ratha* series, and the tales of Rick Raccoon and Scarlett Fox in *Ranger Rick* magazine.

She graduated from Brigham Young University in 2006 and currently resides in the Wild West with her husband and his cat, who was kind enough to adopt her.

Hints of fantasy and science fiction always sneak into whatever she's writing.

For more info about Danielle and her upcoming books, visit *www.PixelvaniaPublishing.com*.

89416741R00124

Made in the USA
San Bernardino, CA
24 September 2018